MEET ME
AT
HEAVEN'S
GATE

ISBN 978-1-5272-4906-6

To contact the author email: lornastennett7@gmail.com

CONTENTS

APPENDIX

RECIPES IN "MEET ME AT HEAVEN'S GATE"

CHAPTER 1

Young fruits were beginning to peep through their pods. Merla had just emerged from the plane into the open air and having cleared customs, exited the small airport. It was still early morning. She was tempted to get into one of the taxicabs lined outside, but as her destination was a long distance away and as the bus she needed was right at the terminal, she decided to take the bus. Saving valuable money she could use more wisely was a valid and sensible decision, she thought. As she got on the bus with her bags and case, she aimed for the back seat. People stared at her as if she just landed from another planet. She looked different to the other passengers; her attire was definitely foreign. The bus made its way through the improvised country roads and as it sped along, clouds of dust obscured the rear window. As it rattled along, it passed through a bustling market town. Early shoppers and market stallholders had already started trading. The noise of music blaring and people shouting complemented the hustle and bustle of the town. The bus recommenced its speeding as they left the town, and Merla surrendered to her reflective mood, thinking while observing the beautiful countryside with its yellow-blossomed trees, contrasting against the green hillside.

She was going to see, her baby, who was now 3 years old. It was two years ago that she had left her daughter with her relative, Aunt Bess, who was known for her kindness, not just within the family circle, but also within the community. Merla kept in touch periodically, always enclosing money with her letters, but this gesture did not compensate for the guilt she now felt at having left her baby, and on top of all this, the infrequency of her contact with her baby daughter and her Aunt. The next stop was hers.

As the bus got nearer and nearer, her guilt was reinforced with self-loathing and doubts: "Could I have done things differently? Am I the only mother who was so wicked as to leave her child for a better life?" "Why did I not come for her sooner?" "Oh my God, I hope she'll know me". "I hope my baby was happy with Aunt B". "I hope they loved her like they loved me". "Have they really forgiven me?" "Will I really be able to cope?" She closed her eyes and prayed silently. "Oh my God, please forgive me. Please guide me to make the right decisions." The bus came to an abrupt stop.

"Mangrove District!" The bus driver shouted.

She alighted the bus with great poise though her suitcase, parcels and handbag tried their hardest to disrupt her deportment. Without helping, the driver impatiently looked on, with the unutterable message of "*Why are you taking so long to get off the bus - foreigner?*" Already she had now begun to look bedraggled. The midday sun was now beating down on her head and shoulders unmercifully. In the distance, figures of men were barely visible, toiling in the fields. Her footprints made a trail on the hot melting asphalt. She was now very tired; even more tired when she realised the house was at least another quarter of a mile away. Although the house was in sight, there was a steep hill to negotiate. She was out of practice with all this walking, but even more so in the heat and her shoes. "All these bags and pans..." she moaned, "I wished I hadn't bought all these things". "Serves you right. Why didn't you just bring money instead?" "You know why you brought these things with you". She rhetorically answered herself. "Half the stuff you need isn't going to be available on the shop shelves in this part of the world". Maybe a small thing, but she realised how she had changed. Merla remembered when she was living there she could not always buy soap as the shop sometimes ran out of this basic requirement. That experience had reminded her to bring soaps and other toiletries, just in case... She had been buying things and stocking up for months so she was unaware of how many things she had acquired for her journey. She stopped to rest under a wide-branched tree - full of maturity and permanence - the same tree that was there in her youth, back in her mother's and grandmother's days. She thought how strange it was that, unlike the town, which was a transient place, the countryside never changed. Life, people, nature, buildings seem to remain the same. Even the precarious shacks and makeshift houses perching on a hill remain the same, stoically defying hurricanes, tropical storms, and whatever the weather threw at them. It was as if the people and the place stubbornly refused to change. As she rested, she looked around, and smells reminiscent of her childhood came flooding back. She turned her head and looked up at the steep hill, which seemed to rise up to heaven, like a rambler's route to its Maker. She remembered even as a toddler, being able to run up and down that hill without any assistance, never falling over.

"As a child I used to be able to run up and down this hill, without any shoes on my feet and without any problem", she pondered. This was the second indication that she was not only getting older, but she had changed significantly. As she rested, one of the local girls approached her, grinning broadly, with a toddler tugging at her dress.

"Hello Dorothy", Merla uttered formally.

"Hello Miss Merla". Merla not only felt a little uncomfortable about being called "Miss" as this seemed to age her but she realised it was an indication of her status in the area and subconsciously Dorothy felt subservient to her, even although they were nearly the same age. This was because of the status bestowed on Aunt Bess and the fact that Merla had travelled.

"How're you keeping?" "You've grown a big young woman, eh? Whose baby is that?" She switched into a patois (broken English) to make her sound more natural and familiar to Dorothy.

"His name's Carl. He's mine", she replied ruefully.

Quick to forget her own mistake and looking sanctimonious, Merla looked shocked and retorted, "But how can that be when only the other day you were in junior school?"

In a burst of laughter Dorothy said, "I had him when I was 15 but in November I'll be 17!" She said this proudly as if it was a ripe old age.

Changing the subject Merla asked, "How's your mum?"

"Today is market day so she won't be home till late".

"Is she still selling fish, fry fish?" Merla asked.

"Yes, but things bad at the moment. When things get bad, she sells fruits, fried dumplings, and drops and all kinds of things to make extra money. It's more work though."

"What about you? - What are you doing with yourself?" asked Merla.

This question caught Dorothy off-guard and after a brief silence, she said. "Well ..... Sometimes I go to the market with me mum. Carl's father gives what he can when he can, and if he feels like it. One day a week, I do some washing and ironing for a teacher woman down the road. Life's tough but we are surviving - just about though. Does Mrs B know you're coming today?"

Merla thought it was an odd question. "No - it's a surprise." "They know me - unpredictable. Well must go now. If your hands weren't so full I would've asked you to give me a hand with my cases."

"I would Miss Merla but I have to meet Tony, Carl's father. He promised some money and I don't want to give him any excuse. You know what I mean?"

Merla didn't know Tony, but she suspected he was one of the local playboys who chatted up the local naïve young girls, hung around dance hall places, had several girls, making out they were the only love in their lives, got them pregnant and then abandoned them. The girls would then have trouble getting money from him to support their child.

"OK, I understand. Take care of yourself...and your baby Carl".

As Dorothy faded into the distance, Merla reflected on herself and the other girls her age and older; these girls growing up all seemed to fall into the same trap. They hadn't seen life; they saw what the consequences were from other girls' mistakes, yet still fell in the same trap. They had not seen life, yet they burdened themselves down with a baby. What was so annoying was that these girls had such low self-esteem, they didn't believe they were good enough and couldn't see beyond their immediate surroundings. The boys complimented them and they believed them. The boys selfishly refused to use the free condoms and the girls acquiesced to try and keep them. A baby came along and before long, they had three or four; then they couldn't do much with their lives as the odds were stacked against them. They couldn't look after themselves yet they created more mouths to feed and before long, they were 'baby mother' to a series of boys and men who promised them the earth under the sheets, yet never delivered because they had no jobs or were simply irresponsible and /or playboys. The dichotomy of this sorry state of affair is the village was still highly conservative and frowned upon having children out of wedlock. Subconsciously, having a child before marriage must have weighed heavily on Merla's mind.

"Idiots! Why do they fall for the same old trick? These men are always promising the earth to these young girls without a hope in hell of keeping their promise. They can't help themselves, how on earth are they going to help you!" She uttered angrily. "Nothing ever changes in this place".

She regained her composure and remembered she had to complete her journey. There were only a few more trees and shacks and Aunt Bess's house was now much closer. She was now very tired and her feet started to ache as they were now swollen in the heat and no longer fitted properly in her shoes.

"What's the matter with you Merla - you getting too fragile to carry heavy bags and what's it with the heat; the climate hasn't changed, pull yourself together or Aunt B will think you're *[1]*pulling style on her*. Again, she reflected, "Imagine I cannot even walk up the hill and I used to run up and down without any trouble. Could it be that I'm getting old?" So peaceful now, the distinct sound that the river made as it meandered through the woods brought back memories of communal bathing and washday. While reflecting she thought it was a hard life, but paradoxically as a child that period was full of innocence and joy.

As she recommenced her journey, she pondered.

---

1   Jamaican term for showing off.

"Please God, give me the strength to do what I am doing. I pray I am doing the right thing. I know that there are going to be problems - when I am at work or if she is sick, what am I going to do? What happens if I lose my job or have money problems?" As she walked, she counter-argued that in any case, if Jenny was removed from the scenario, she would still have to face the same problems.

The house perched on top of the hill in a precarious manner. A few alterations had been undertaken since Merla had left as the bare wooded outer walls were now painted and an extension added to the side. It was now one of the more *affluent* houses in the area, which subliminally helped to increase the respect bestowed on Aunt Bess and her family.

Aunt Bess was about 50 years old but because of hard work, she was a spindly-looking woman, very dignified, but her quiet demeanour underlied a stoic, industrious woman. Her husband, 5 years older than her, was a stout, strong farmer, who worked on his farm until late evening. He always worked hard to provide for the family. They got married comparatively late in life, but coming from a Christian family, she had to marry a Christian man. On leaving college, both worked in an international bank when they were young, but got a modest redundancy package when their bank merged and cut staff. This modest windfall helped to resurrect the family farm. As the elder sister, when Merla's mother died of cancer prematurely at the young age of 30, Aunt Bess naturally assumed responsibility for Merla who was only five when she lost her mother. Being a devout Christian, Aunt Bess was extremely kind and a constant stream of children was always in her care. In a way, they were rich and as Aunt Bess would say, 'very blessed', as having a farm, there was never any shortage of food. Only a few basic things were bought from the shop: things such as meat, soap, and bread. Bess was always an optimist and trusted in the Lord. She maintained that another child would not make a big difference, so Merla joined the family.

Merla knocked on the door, but there was no reply, so she rapped on the glass window. There was still no reply so she turned the handle and walked in.

"Is anybody home?" She called.

The voice disturbed her daughter who woke abruptly and started to cry. Seeing her daughter for the first time in two years, brought tears to Merla's eyes. Merla was overwhelmed with emotions: she couldn't believe her daughter had grown so big in such a, what she thought was, short period of time. Her immediate thought was also who the hell she thought she was intruding into the child's life by waking her, making her cry and coming back into her life. Merla crept over to her, hugged her tightly and in between kisses she said, "It's your mummy my darling, where's Aunt Bess?" She took her in her arms and ventured to the back of the house.

Aunt Bess was outside in the back taking a nap under a tree in her favourite chair. It took a few seconds before Aunt Bess realised she was not dreaming and it was really Merla.

"Merla! You didn't tell me you were coming". Immediately she rose and said, "Let me get you a drink. When did you arrive in the country? You look tired girl. Are you hungry? I haven't a thing in the house to eat. If you'd told me you were coming I would......"

"That's all right - I'm not hungry but I will have the drink. Don't worry yourself."

"Pull up the stool and come over here while I get your drink. Rest yourself. You see how your daughter has grown?"

"So I see - what're you feeding her on?"

"It's the green banana and porridge for breakfast, especially since she has a mouth full of teeth!" Aunt Bess replied with a big grin on her face as she went to get the drink.

As she cut the limes for the drink she mumbled, "These limes - they're no good - dry and nothing but seeds". I haven't any ice but I did run the pipe for a while".[2]

"Thanks, that's fine" said Merla.

---

2   Showing hospitality, as water is a precious commodity

"So, how's life girl?" "What breeze blows you down here? You're always springing surprises on me."

It could be guilt, oversensitivity or paranoia but Merla detected an ambiguity in that statement, as she always felt guilty that she let her Aunt and the family down by getting pregnant; not only was she not married, but also *before* she completed her education, she had a child. Coming from a Christian home, that also brought shame on the family. She quickly changed the subject.

"Who painted the front? It looks really nice. I see you have extended it also".

"Mr Johnson; you remember Mr Johnson don't you? His daughter went to the same school as you and I think it's around the same time".

"What's her name?"

"Daphne".

"The name rings a bell".

"Mr Johnson was a fast worker. He also put on the extra room to the side. No messing about like some of the other useless builders or young people who say they're going to do a job and take all year to finish it off….. if they ever finish. They just want the money and God help you if you dare pay them before they finish the job. Mr Johnson finished the job in about one month, no fuss and he cleared up everything after each day. I am very satisfied with what he did. He even ordered the material as well".

"I don't expect there's much call for a builder or painter round here so you must expect him to do the job properly. How many can afford the paint, let alone a builder?"

"He wasn't that expensive either. His daughter is doing well. She went to university and is now getting married to a fine young man she met there. He's some big shot. You want to see the car they drove in to meet her family the other day - definitely money people". This was another unintentional reminder of her failings.

"I met Dorothy on my way here. Everybody turn big in such a short space of time. How are Mrs Mac and her husband? Are they still living at the same place?"

"My dear I couldn't tell when last I saw them. Your poor Aunt is going through her change of life and the heat does not help; it slows me down and makes me irritable. I can't get around to seeing everybody the way I used to. The only time I see anybody is when we go to church. The Macs used to come to church every Saturday but Mr Mac had a stroke. I don't know if you know but Mr Mac was much older than his wife. Pastor Morris visits them regularly and they pray. It's a shame, but what can we poor mortals do? The Lord never gives us more than we can bear. God will help them. ......He always does." This statement now convinced Merla that she was doing the right thing to take her daughter with her as having to care for Jenny may also be putting a strain on Aunt Bess's health.

While they talked, Merla held her baby daughter in her arms, cuddling her, and stroking her forehead and cheeks. Not seeing her daughter for a long time and being more mature, she was now really appreciating motherhood. Although Aunt Bess was a loving care-giver, no doubt Jenny was feeling the love of her natural mother and she instinctively reciprocated by cuddling her mother. It was clear they were both enjoying the moment. As they talked, a gentle breeze passed through the leaves, creating a swishing sound. Some trees were already laden with fruits although it was the latter part of spring. Their talking disturbed a lizard causing it to make a sudden detour into the hedgerow.

"So when are you going back?" Aunt Bess queried.

Merla had butterflies in her stomach and tried hard to recall what she had rehearsed to tell them so her answer was grateful and pleasant.

"I'm here until next Friday."

"Jenny is growing up fast and soon if I'm not careful, she will be big and won't know her mother and I'll have missed her growing up. Time is speeding by so quickly and she will have grown a big girl before too long. I've decided to take her back with me. It's not something I could say in a letter and that's why I didn't tell you I was coming. I know you all love her and Jenny loves you and I wouldn't have left her with anyone else. I am so grateful to you and Uncle. You'll never know how indebted I feel towards you and Uncle Harry."

Merla reflected on her own childhood and although she was happy and Aunt Bess and Uncle Harry treated her like their own child, it was always in the back of her mind that Bess wasn't her birth mother and she wondered what would her relationship had been like with her birth mother. She was adamant that Jenny should not have such experience, doubt, and feeling about her.

"My flat's not all that big, but last year I got a decent bonus and I used the opportunity to purchase the flat instead of renting. I have a mortgage on it, but I try to make it as pleasant and comfortable as possible. Things are not cheap but I manage surprisingly well.

Pausing for a short while after digesting this sudden news, Bess said, "I know how you feel. It's going to be lonely without her and I will miss her, but I understand. It will be better for you and her. How are you going to manage when you are at work or when she gets sick? Do you have anyone to help you?"

"Don't worry, I've plans, and if things go as planned, it will be just fine. I'll have to manage. I won't be the first person to face this situation. Its difficult to sort out everything as I don't know what we are going to face but if the worse comes to the worst, I can always bring her back, cant I"? Merla said with a wry smile.

Protectively Aunt Bess said, "Of course, but Merla you don't know how to rough it. You haven't that experience and neither has Jenny. You're not used to rushing around after work, cooking, and caring for someone else. Supposed she gets sick - what're going to do"?

Merla expected some helpful advice and warnings of potential problems, but not this much. She realised the suddenness of the situation and Aunt Bess shock at, not only seeing her, but now being told Jenny would no longer be with her.

"I can't forecast all the difficulties that I'll have to face, but people cope, don't they? I'll have to learn to cope just like everybody else. Before coming over, I asked a woman living near to me and she's agreed to help me by keeping Jenny while I'm at work. I haven't discussed money yet with her, but she reassured me she would only charge a set reasonable amount each week so I don't have to break my neck to get home from work in time to collect her. Eventually, by the time she starts school, I will be able to rearrange the living accommodation and sponsor a girl from the country to look after her and collect her from school for me. That person can do jobs around the house while I'm at work and if she wants to go to evening classes, and improve her life by educating herself, she'll get the opportunity. Quite a few people would jump at the opportunity to get free board and lodgings, and a reasonable amount each week, not to mention a chance to get a visa".

"It's going to be hard, and I don't know if it'll be right for Jenny, but as I say, I understand your concerns".

"I was waiting till I get settled and until things improve for me financially but, it's the most settled I'm going to be, so I have to be brave as I'm never going to have everything I want. I hope that out of all this experience, we will both learn from it and we will grow together. I hope you understand my point".

"Yes, of course. If things don't work out for you, and her, I will gladly take her back". "You must be hungry. There is nothing in the house to eat but I could always open that tin of corned beef that you brought with you. Cook it with some dumplings and that piece of yam. What do you say?"

"……. OK, let me give you a hand in the kitchen".

Gently Merla freed Jenny from her arms and went into the kitchen with Aunt B.

Most country people cooked outside - not only was it cooler and kept the food smell out of the house, but it was cheaper and more practical cooking on an open barbecue style fire. Aunt Bess's kitchen was out of the ordinary, quite luxurious for a country house. Granted it was an *afterthought*, added after the house was built, but this was usual for most people in the area who *saved* for an extension. As they saved more money, they expanded their homes. The extension kitchen walls were constructed with different kinds of wood. This is borne out in the subtle difference in the colouring and textures. It is possible that this was the economic way of building the extension by buying what was available. There were several cupboards handmade by a local carpenter, with a sink and a cooker. Aunt Bess was very proud of her kitchen as she could go into the kitchen at nights without problem.

"You can make the dumplings while I slice the onions and look after the corned beef". "Your dumplings always taste superb - much better than mine", said Merla.

"No, it's too early to put on the corned beef; all the oil will dry out. Just stay with me and I'll do it. It won't take me long." Aunt Bess enjoyed being the host and loved cooking but it was doubly enjoyable cooking for her niece, who was like a daughter to her.

"Where's the yam - I'll peel while I'm talking to you".

"It's under the sink, in that box", Aunt Bess pointed.

While they talked, Aunt Bess kneaded and with each 'end of sentence', she reinforced the dough with an extra kneading. They were going to be extra tight and heavy and Merla would be taking optimism to a new level if she thought she could eat more than two!

"How do you get your dumplings so round, tight and smooth Aunt Bess? Mine are always soft and full of *dimples* when they touch the boiling water. Yours are always tasty and firm."

"Girl, I've had more practice than you. In addition, you need time to develop these skills. Pass me some water in that cup please." She tipped a tiny drop of water in the bowl to remove the extra flour round the bowl's edge.

"You young people nowadays have life so easy, so many take-aways, and restaurants. You know when I was eleven, I was expected to help my mother wash and cook, look after my younger brothers and sister"? "I remember every Monday morning down at the river we'd go with our bundles of clothes to wash. We took the day off from school to help our mothers. I don't think they do that nowadays as the school authorities would be on to the parents. Looking back on that time, I can't remember the drudgery and how hard this was. I just remember we had children our own age to laugh with while we worked and we got a day off from school. I don't really remember why we had to be down by the river so early but we woke up at the crack of dawn. I remember hating the early Monday morning wakes. Lord, how I hated these *dawn raids* by my mother on Monday mornings." "Bessie, wake up! I still remember vividly those words".

"Bessie, mum says wake up," one of my other sibling would reiterate.

"Shut your mouth, leave me alone!" I would bellow back at my siblings covering my head with the pillow. We sometimes had the privilege of having a lie-in if mother went early and dad would supervise the biggest breakfast, with cornmeal porridge and a big piece of hard dough bread. We would then make our way to the river later on in the morning, but that didn't happen too often as dad was usually on his way to work much earlier".

By now, the yam and dumplings were almost cooked, so it was time to prepare the corned beef.

"Anyway, like it or not, we had to go. We were soon on our way to the river with our clothes. On the way, we usually met other women and children heading to the same destination as us. We resembled a convoy of women soldiers marching, but our *uniforms* were far from glamorous, usually the full skirts and off the shoulder blouses. Our headgear was the bundle or pan with clothes. We all converged at the same place: the riverbank. These Monday morning rendezvous served as a double purpose: to wash clothes and as a social gathering where the women caught up with the latest parish gossips and news. They didn't need to read newspapers in these areas. While they talked and laughed, the swishing and scrubbing on the washboard served as an accompaniment. Clothes with stubborn stains they spread either on a rock, or on a piece of zinc sheet, to be bleached by the gloriously hot sun."

A mischievous smile adorned Aunt Bess's face.

"You know what we children used to do? Peep on the women bathing. So help us if we were caught!"

Merla struggled to picture Bess as a mischievous young girl.

Bess quickly returned to the subject. "We didn't use any of this modern washing powder. A bar of soap used to do a better job and go much further. We washed clothes, bathed, and cooked by the river. Each woman had her territory on that riverbank and in the river. This was a kind of unspoken agreement. Laughter, gossiping, and shouting competed with the deafening sound the cascading water made as it pushed its way downstream. The overhanging trees that lined the riverbank served as an umbrella when the heat became unbearable. By the afternoon, hair washed, body clean, clothes clean and tired women made their way home with young children tugging at their skirt. The rest of the week we went to the local parish schools".

"Well, it sounds more fun to me than hard work" Merla said.

"You must be joking! You have no idea what hard work is girl".

By now, the food was ready.

"I'll have two dumplings please", said Merla.

"Are you sure? Is that all? I thought you were hungry."

"I am …… but you know, I couldn't eat more than two of your dumplings".

"This is a lovely piece of yam - look how pretty it is. Have this piece".

"You want me to get fat - don't you?"

"You could do with a bit of fat on you". Aunt Bess said endearingly, "Look at your arms!"

They took the food and drinks and went into the dining room with Jenny toddling behind.

"Here's yours sweetheart".

"Can she manage dumplings like that?"

"Of course she can," Aunt Bess retorted.

By now, they were so hungry they ate in silence, but it wasn't an uncomfortable silence. The clang of the cutlery against the plates interrupted this peace now and again. Aunt Bess was the first to finish so she asked Merla if she wanted any more or if she wanted a mango to round off the meal.

"Um, this is delicious". I still don't know how you can make the humble corned beef taste so good".

"You were starving plus you can't really go wrong with corned beef", Aunt Bess modestly replied. "Maybe the oil had something to do with it. Fresh coconut oil, that's the only thing I can think of."

"No, truthfully, it was lovely".

"I'll cook some ackee and salt-fish tomorrow or Friday. By the way when are you returning?" Bess asked.

"I must get back by next Friday. I will have just over a week to sort out Jenny and myself. I need to do a bit of shopping for her and get some food. It's not like the country you know. You can't pick fruit or ask the neighbour for something. Everybody minds their own business", said Merla.

"Why can't you ask your neighbour?"

"You must be joking! The town people aren't like you country folks you know. They are proud, greedy, and not very friendly. Mark you, if you do anything wrong, they know and they will tell the whole world! They look down on things like that - think you are begging because you can't afford it; and they yearn for what the other person has. They will do anything to impress their neighbour. They're not very nice people. You talk to them to be friendly but you have to be very careful who you tell your business to", added Merla.

"My dear you have to be careful who you confide in wherever you live. Things are getting bad everywhere. People have changed here as well. They go to church every week and they say they worship God, but they are getting as selfish and greedy; they don't serve the same Lord as I do! Thank God, it's the same people here in this part of the country that I know from childhood. They know you and we are all in the same boat, so we help each other. The problem is getting worse here though, as we have many newcomers coming in and the ones who went to live in town and have returned. They come back with bad habits and attitudes. Fewer of them go to church and even if they are believers, they don't behave the way the Lord wants them to behave. Their faith has gone, and with that, they become selfish. If only they had kept their faith, He would have granted them whatever they needed, but no, they have to get everything immediately. If they cannot afford it, they rely on a human being or they steal and lie. "*Thou shall not covet thy neighbour's house.*" I don't know what this world is coming to. It's such a shame. By the way, when did you last go to church?" Aunt Bess blurted all this out in one breath.

Merla racked her brains, wondering how the subject of religion cropped into the conversation. She should have known better that eventually with Aunt Bess, the subject is never far away. She was now thinking very hard as to how she could smooth over the question as a wrong answer could have a negative reaction and she didn't want to upset or lie to Aunt Bess. It was also against Merla's principle to lie, especially about a thing like God and the church.

The long pause confirmed Aunt Bess's rhetorical question.

"You can't remember, can you? Oh Merla, you aren't going to bring up Jenny to be a non-believer are you?"

Merla didn't want to fall out with her Aunt as she loved and respected her.

She was however beginning to feel stifled and it brought back some negative memories.

"It's not always easy to go to church when you go to work in a big city you know. Remember in the short space of time I worked and went to night school, and by the weekend I am shattered, but I still believe in God and I read my Bible. My upbringing hasn't disappeared you know. Of course I will tell Jenny what's good and what's bad; teach her about God. She will go to a church close to us when we settle down. I don't agree that the church is the only place where she will learn about the code of morality. Take the people who go to church for example, some of them are the biggest hypocrites. They are devils during the week and weekends they pray for forgiveness".

Aunt Bess went silent.

Merla added. "Look , I admit that I haven't been to church for a while but its difficult when you work and you have household chores to do at the weekend. It's the time I catch up on the housework and relax. That doesn't make me less of a Christian and a good person. I am a believer, I pray every night, and He's answering all my prayers. I couldn't survive without Him. He gives me hope and I am a strong believer".

Aunt Bess looked down on Jenny who was now quite bored with their inattentiveness and went off to play across the other side of the room.

"I think it's important, especially for children, to go to church. God and the church will give them mental and moral stability to last a lifetime. You can't go wrong with God", added Aunt Bess.

"What I'm saying is, there are other things I hope to teach her as well. Like having self-respect, doing good deeds for others, but unlike what the Bible says, 'NOT turning the other cheek! That hasn't got us far at all," said Merla.

"You can get all that teaching by sending her to church and teaching her to read the Bible", retorts Aunt Bess.

"Exactly, she can get all the religious education she needs by reading the

Bible", said Merla.

"I cannot believe I am hearing this from you Merla! The City has changed you". Retiringly Aunt Bess ended the conversation by humming her reply to *'What a friend we have in Jesus'*.

Religion is such an emotive subject, it never fails to start a conversation or argument; it never fails to bring out the best or the worse in people.

Merla closed the subject by reassuring Aunt Bess not to worry, as she would ensure Jenny goes to church, giving her a Christian upbringing.

They hugged each other and Aunt Bess added, "I know you are a sensible young woman and you want the best for Jenny. I know you have your own mind; you're a good person and you won't follow those heathens who see the devil as their god".

Merla retreated to the corner where Jenny was playing with her toys. While they played, Aunt Bess busied herself with the washing up in the kitchen.

Time seems to move very slowly in the country, but a good hour had passed and evening was now approaching. When Aunt Bess' children, Eddie 14 and Gloria 13 had finished school for the day, they made a detour to visit their father's farm. When they finally arrived home, they sauntered tiredly into the room, not expecting to see Merla. Joy and excitement over-powered their tiredness on seeing Merla.

"Merla!" they hugged and kissed her.

"Aren't you big and you Eddie? You've turned man in such a short time!"

"Where's your father?" Aunt Bess queried.

"Oh, he told us to go on; he wanted to finish planting the yam tubers before the weekend. He didn't know what time he'd be home but said not to wait for him to eat".

"We've already had dinner but food is outside for you. Share out and leave some for dad".

"Did he give you anything to bring home?"

"Oh yes, here's the yam", Eddie said handing her a whopper of a yam. Nothing can beat growing your own yam, as they tend to be sweeter, nicer, and most importantly, enormous. "He was going to get some fish this morning but the ones down at Mr Chin's shop looked so whingy, he didn't bother in the end".

"It's a good job I wasn't depending on the fish. That's why I like to have some provisions in the cupboard. You can't go wrong with tinned mackerel and corned beef in the cupboard". A lesson learnt from Aunt Bess's mother that it was important to be prepared when it comes to food, it was important to think about a rainy day.

"I think he knew and that's why he didn't bother to buy the fish", retorted Eddie.

"So Eddie, do you like going to the farm?" asked Merla.

An obvious pause indicated that he was not sure how to answer this question in front of his mother. If he said 'yes', he was inviting spontaneous fits of laughter, not only from Aunt Bess, but also from Gloria. A 'no' may indicate laziness.

He opted for the safest diplomatic answer. "Sometimes…….. ".

"Like when?" teased Gloria.

Eddie gave her a filthy look. Merla sensed the question was not a tactful one and to avoid an argument, she intervened to quash an unpleasant squabble.

"I know what you mean. Sometimes I don't feel like going to work, I don't feel like doing something, but I have to get on with it. Another day I get up with a spring in my step. Eddie and Gloria, you won't always want to do what you have to: sometimes you have to force yourself, but that's a positive discipline to learn."

"Those two can't get on at all; also him and his father. This house is a constant battleground. I'm caught in the middle, I feel like a ……….. What do you call the man in the ring when two boxers fighting?"

"A referee," replied Merla. "But Aunty you have to understand, it's their age as well, they are rebelling against everything. They are rebelling about getting older, finding where they are in the pecking order; it's natural". Becoming little adults mean they feel they know everything and are right and sometimes they feel out of control". Merla matter-of-factly retorted while she opened her bag. [It seemed odd that Merla would be advising Bess about children's behaviour considering Bess was more experienced, but somehow Merla was more aware of how modern day children behaved.]

"Yes, I am the referee. I pray to God everyday to bring Eddie and his father closer together".

Rummaging in her suitcase Merla said, "Here Gloria, try on this dress. I didn't realise how big you'd grown so I hope it fits. The trousers should fit Eddie, as I knew if they was too long, we could shorten them easily. One of my neighbours has a son who is around your age so I took his measurements and bought the next size up".

They both scampered out of the room to try on their presents after thanking Merla.

"I bought this about a month ago. I saw it in the local department store and I thought it would suit you". Removing the box cover, she unveiled a beautiful beige hat. "Do you like it?" she asked Aunt Bess.

"Child it's lovely; really beautiful. Just right for church and it will go with so many outfits. You know I am grateful, but this is your home; you don't have to buy all these things for us when you are coming home. This will go just nice with a cream dress I have. I think I'll wear them this Saturday. I'll be a proper dress-puss this week." Aunt Bess smiled and thanked Merla.

Mimicking how a well turned out woman would walk, with her nose in the air, Aunt Bess tried on the hat and asked. "Have I got it round the right way?"

Merla tilted it slightly to one side and remarked, "I'm glad you like it. It was a safe bet anyway, especially the colour. There's no way I could've got it wrong when you wear hats to church and this colour will go with most of your outfits."

Dusk was now setting in and Uncle Harry wearily made his way up the hill. Exhaustion dictated his pace. He made his way straight for the bathroom to wash his well-worn hands, took off his shoes and refreshed himself without realising he had a visitor. Bess was already in the kitchen, warming the dinner. Harry walked into the sitting room.

"Oh my Lord - how are you keeping m'dear!?" He greeted Merla with a hug and a broad smile. "I didn't know you were coming home!"

"So, so. I thought I'd give you folks a surprise."

"You're looking good m'dear. Lord, I worked hard today. I had to do as much as possible as it's nearly the weekend and I want to start clearing and digging the spot near the river by next week. It's a wilderness! So, how long are you staying? I know you; you're not a country girl".

"'Until next Friday. I have to get back to sort out Jenny and straighten out myself. I have to do all that in a week and then I'm back at work".

Uncle Harry still hadn't caught on when Merla mentioned 'sort out Jenny' and just went into the kitchen to see what was for dinner. He ate his dinner in the kitchen with his wife keeping his company and after returned to the room.

Merla was surprised that there was no reaction to her comment about Jenny, so she repeated, "I'm taking Jenny with me. Before long she won't know her mum and there is never going to be a right time."

Not surprisingly as Uncle Harry, so placid and the master of understatements, just said, "You must know your own mind ......if you think it's a good idea..." The subject ended abruptly and they went on to other topics.

They talked and joked and by now it was 9 o'clock, which was very late for country folks who had to get up very early to do their work before the disabling midday heat. A lack of evening entertainment and the dearth of good programmes on television and the radio were also a deciding factor.

Merla wasn't ready for bed but as everybody was getting ready for bed, she also retired, but sleep eluded her. She laid there looking out of the curtain-less window. The *peenies* or fireflies danced in the dark, brightening the sky with their flickering lights. The shrill of nocturnal birds, the croaking lizards, and other nocturnal creatures and insects all contributed to a chorus of weird noises. Merla eventually fell asleep; but was awakened by the crowing of a loud cock very early, and it wasn't long before scavenging dogs started to bark. By now, the morning sun forced its way through the window. She had forgotten how noisy the country could be. Most of the noises in the cities were from man-made objects such as the radio or television, cars and buses, car horns, operated by humankind, but in a perverted way, they were controllable, unlike the country where the noises were from animals, birds and creatures; humans had less control over their behaviour. She laid there thinking how she would plan the day, as she didn't want to waste the time she had with Aunt Bess and the rest of the family.

"I think I'll clean up the house today", she thought. Merla was aware this might present a little difficulty, as she didn't want to offend Aunt Bess; that she thought the house wasn't clean enough or that she was getting above her station in life. It wasn't that the place wasn't clean but more because it was dated and full of clutter. Gifts and ornaments collected over several years, and things that Aunt Bess refused to part with, all added to the clutter. The display cabinet, which was full of bone china crockery, glasses with fancy patterns, and other things, always saving for 'best', that had never been used or even looked at, now had additional layers of dust, which had become a permanent feature on the objects. It was not the helper's fault that they were into such a state, but Aunt Bess' refusal to let anyone touch her precious ornaments. Merla made herself a cup of mint tea quietly so she didn't wake the others in the house.

It wasn't long before Uncle Harry was also up and about, getting himself ready for the farm. As a hard-working man, Uncle Harry didn't bother about breakfast as he knew he could get a cooked lunch from a neighbour near the farm, or a higgler (a term which still survived in the Caribbean to describe someone selling at the roadside or in the market) selling food en route to the farm. He was more anxious to start the day early before the sun beat down on his back, so he got up, sorted out himself for work and it wasn't long before he was saying goodbye to all early birders who were awake. Aunty Bess woke Eddie, asking him to run to the corner shop not far down the road to get milk, as she wanted to make some porridge for breakfast.

Merla thought to herself "How on earth am I going to manage this coming week?" She had forgotten how country folks, especially her Aunt, were laid back about the essential matters such as milk in the house. She was now used to a more structured lifestyle where she went to the supermarket weekly or fortnightly to ensure she never ran out of provisions. Merla got back into bed when she saw Jenny waking up and put her into the bed so they could cuddle up together. That warm and loving feeling was new to Merla so she relished the moment and told herself this would be the beginning of a loving relationship with her daughter.

Aunt Bess started to prepare the porridge when she saw Eddie making his way back from the shop. She made a big pot of cornmeal porridge for everyone, sweetening it with condensed milk and vanilla pod. The taste of the real vanilla pod heightened the flavour. Gloria and Eddie were now dressed for school and they quickly had their breakfast. If they missed that school bus there wouldn't be another one until the next day. This scenario prompted a speedy farewell.

Although she didn't want to leave Jenny, Merla started to make a list of the things she would buy for the week so she could give Aunt Bess a break from shopping. She would return in a taxicab. While she wrote, she enquired as to whether the woman who sold green banana, pumpkin, etc. was still selling outside the supermarket; and whether the taxi rank was still across the road from the supermarket.

Jenny stayed with Aunt Bess as Merla made her way to get the bus or to hail a cab as it approached at breakneck speed. Unnerving as the latter was, she knew how irregular the bus was, so she had to take her life in her hands if she wanted to get to the shops early. She held out her hand as a taxi approached with people already in the back. It stopped and she went into the front passenger seat, greeting the others with a haughty "Good morning". There was no need to ask where people were going; they were all heading for downtown where all the supermarkets, offices, shops, and people worked. The roads were full of manholes but that didn't stop the taxi drivers from driving at breakneck speed, as if they were on a racetrack. The usual passengers were used to this form of travel, but for the uninitiated, it was a frightening experience.

As they scrambled out of the taxi, Merla felt a tremendous relief at getting out, not just unscathed, but alive! As she walked along, she dashed into those familiar shops she once visited. Eventually she got to the Metro supermarket. She had not expected to see guards in the entrance of the supermarket so that was new to her but she took the trolley and got out her list ready for business.

On top of this list was meat. She wanted to buy good quality food to spoil the family while she was there. It's not so much because Aunt Bess and family couldn't afford good quality meat; they just refused to pay extortionate prices for meat and food as they were far too frugal. They were aware that these things were sometimes available in the country at a fraction of the price, especially plantains and yam. The priority was drinks. Merla picked up fresh juice and bottled water, aware that she had to carry the bags back along the long road home. Even with a taxicab, it was going to be difficult. In the back of her mind she wanted to buy a far from light pumpkin and large green bananas outside the supermarket so she needed caution as to how much more she could put in that trolley. The taxi rank was close by so it wasn't long before Merla was returning home. She was determined not to share the cab with strangers this time, even if the taxi fare was exorbitant. She couldn't stand the thought of the cab zooming through the narrow country roads to drop off other people, thus lengthening her journey. In addition, Merla didn't feel like talking to strangers that day. The taxi wound its way round the bends like an ambulance or a police car in an emergency. She reminded the driver jokingly she wanted to get to her destination in one piece. His retort was to [3]*'kiss his teeth'*.

"Wow, you bought so much meat, Merla". Aunt Bess commented. "What did you have in mind to cook today?"

"Maybe you could cook the beef today and tomorrow I'll cook some chicken, but with my special jerk sauce, which I didn't know I would have found here but surprisingly I did".

Aunt Bess quickly packed out the grocery and prepared the kitchen for her culinary delight, while Merla rested on the veranda with Jenny. Jenny was confused and wary as to whom this strange woman was, but within a short period, she began to trust Merla, although now and again there was this awkwardness in her response to her mother's affection. Undeterred, Merla did not care whether or why Jenny responded. She was just happy to try to make up for lost time by showering her with love and attention.

As she rested, she reflected on how much she as a person had changed. "This is not the life for me any more," she thought. I couldn't just sit and watch the world go by every day. How on earth can a human being get up every day to what she considered drudgery?"

Dinnertime coincided with the arrival of Eddie and Gloria from school. The whole family, minus Uncle Harry sat down to dinner, with Aunt Bess gracing the table. The gracing of the table was commonplace and the family took it in turn to say grace. This time Aunt Bess kicked off this ritual with a lengthy prayer, thanking God for the meal and for Merla's presence. Merla always found Aunt Bess' prayers never-ending.

Mealtime hadn't changed: it was the time to catch up on the day's events and to express what each person thought about what was happening in the

---

3   Show contempt and lacking diplomacy.

community and elsewhere. Updating on how school was going featured prominently in their daily discussions. Expressing oneself and participating in conversations was important. It afforded even the youngest person in the family to express their thoughts. It was obvious they were hungry as the platters were clean.

Eddie and Gloria now excused themselves to leave the table and went to their rooms to do their homework.

Merla looked on the bookshelf to see what was available to read as she now thought it was going to be a long evening and night. It was more commonplace to find a full set of the Encyclopaedia Britannica on the bookshelf and although people read books in the Caribbean, the bookshelf was filled with mostly classic books, which were still undisturbed in leather-bound covers. It seemed incongruous and extraordinary that a full set of Charles Dickens, Jane Eyre, Pride and Prejudice books should be on the shelf of a humble country home. Several other paperback classics were also on the shelf, including John Steinbeck's "Grapes of Wrath", and some obscure poetry titles. These books were surely a throwback from a traditional English-based colonial society. A well-worn Bible was also on the shelf with several stickers and markings, indicating chapters and verses worth reading and re-reading. Merla wondered if anyone had read these books or if they were inspirational titles for the children, to expose them to knowledge. Apart from the Bible, she certainly didn't think this was Aunt Bess' reading list but she wondered who in the family would have known about these books. It would have to be a worldly person who was perhaps an academic, perhaps aware of literature to select these books. She browsed through the titles and picked out what she considered an interesting title "The Pearl" by John Steinbeck. This looked thin enough to read and finish while she was there. Spotting a photo album, Merla took this out and started to look through this. The album was bulging with old black and white photographs; some now lost their edges, and others had turned a creamy colour. She looked through the album and recalled some of the ones of her family and of her as a toddler. Photos were not taken regularly in the country as people had more important things to think about, but Aunt Bess made sure her little Brownie always had a roll of film inside the camera, to be developed when she went into town, and just in case she needed to take photos of the family or to have evidence of something.

Merla asked, "Where did you get these books?"

"A teacher woman died and left loads of books and her family was disposing of them so I asked if I could have them, making a donation to the church. At the time, I thought I would start reading them but mainly they were for Eddie and Gloria. In the evenings when they were bored, they could pick up a book. However, as you can see, with the amount of dust collected on them, they haven't been touched. You know you can take the horse to the river, but you can't force it to drink."

Merla continued to look through the album and came across a lovely photograph of Jenny about the age of two. "How old was Jenny here? Was this taken before she went to church"?

"Yes, about two; one Sunday last year, she looked so pretty in her new dress. I had to take a photo of her".

Both women chatted while Jenny lay in her mother's lap. It was now getting dark so the conversation halted so Merla could prepare Jenny for bed. The two women continued their chitchat, catching up on what was happening in their lives. Eddie and Gloria said goodnight to them before showering for bed.

As she retired to bed, Merla took the book "The Pearl" to read. She didn't get past the first four pages when she felt sleepy and dropped off.

The next morning, she woke up to the same noise of the country with the early morning sun peeping through the window. She laid there planning how she would spend the day. She decided to clean the whole house (or as much as she could do on her own) as it will be Friday and cleaning was normally done before the weekend.

"I wonder if there are any rubber gloves - my nails are going to break with the bleach and water getting to my hands. I'll have a look in the bottom drawer in the kitchen when I get up as I won't even tell her I'm going to clean up as Aunt Bess will discourage me from doing this", she thought.

On getting out of bed, Merla prepared breakfast and as the family finished eating, she went straight into planning what room she would start on and in what order.

"I really appreciate what you are going to do for us but do you have to do all this? You will be tired when you return home and as I told you when I want, I can get the cleaner to come round. You make me feel really bad!" said Bess.

"It won't take me long to do, and I am trying to save you money". Why should you pay for something I can easily do within a day?" I'm happy to do this; I'm hardly around to help, so when I want to, please let me."

Aunt Bess knew she wasn't going to win the argument so she retreated to her room to finish dressing and combing her hair. She thought to herself, "She hasn't changed; still stubborn and has to get her own way".

As she took the glasses and china out of the cabinet to clean them, there was a shout from across the room, "Please be careful with those glasses. I've had them for years!"

"I know. They're probably older than me, eh?" shouted Merla.

Answering with a smile, Aunt Bess said, "You know, I think you're right".

While Aunt Bess dressed Jenny, Merla continued with the lounge and now started on the bathroom and she worked through undisturbed. While she worked, she played some music to help her along. She had gotten used to dusting and cleaning with music in the background as it helped her along. "Hope the music isn't too loud for you. Let me know and I'll turn it down!"

"No, it's fine. My place is so quiet in the days when I'm here on my own, it makes a change. I love to listen to the birds singing and occasionally I put on the radio. In any case I'm used to loud music as that man down the road, when he puts on his music, the entire neighbourhood hear it".

Finishing the bathroom, she tackled the kitchen, which was the biggest, as she wanted to clean inside the cupboards as well.

"Tell me something, what does that cleaner do when she comes round? She hasn't touched the inside of the cupboards and drawers. As to the fridge, I don't think she's ever cleaned inside. She probably just does the outside and thinks it is OK. You need to tell her as it looks like she doesn't know it needs to clean. These people weren't taught to clean. They are poor and just think cleaning is not a serious job, so it's understandable but you need to tell her. If you want, I can tell her for you before I leave. It doesn't have to be contentious. I'll be diplomatic but the only problem is once I have gone after a few months, it will be back to normal".

"It's all right - I'll tell her when I see her next", said Aunt Bess.

Merla wondered if Aunt Bess was just fobbing her off with that statement to avoid any confrontation with the cleaner.

The kitchen, now thoroughly cleaned, meant Merla was truly tired so she slumped into the chair on the veranda. Jenny joined her with a book. She was tired but realised this was the new reality. Even when she is tired coming home from work, she would need to find the strength to give time to her daughter.

Aunt Bess now also joined them. "So what exactly do you do at work?"

"Well when I left you guys, I didn't waste time. On arriving in the UK, I got a secretarial job, working in a solicitor's office. After work, I went to evening class to get some legal training. I did a course in proofreading also. It was hard but I did complete the courses and now I am on a better grade, as I am now a legal executive, so now I think I am ready to take the next step. I could devote myself to bettering myself by going to school after work as I only had myself to look after."

"What's a legal executive?"

I am the lawyers' dogsbody. I do a lot of the lawyers' work. A legal executive is a person qualified through training to perform legal work that requires *some* knowledge of the law and legal procedure. I am there to support and make the lawyer's work easier. I couldn't have done this without your help as I was able to go to school in the evenings and although I was tired, I didn't have to think about anyone but myself. I am truly grateful to you and I want you all to be proud of Jenny and me but I haven't finished yet. I still have goals to complete but can't say any more about my next phase as yet".

"You know I care for you both and I know you can do whatever you set your mind to as you are a bright girl. As I said earlier, we will always be there for you and Jenny whenever you need our help".

It was Merla's turn to cook dinner so she prepared the chicken by seasoning with her special sauce. Meanwhile Aunt Bess prepared the fish for tomorrow's dinner. Merla thought, "It's a good job I bought that sauce. There's hardly any seasoning in the cupboard". I must admit the food over here tastes great and so much fresher, so they probably don't really need much seasoning anyway. The two women exchanged culinary ideas and talked as Merla cooked.

"We're going to church tomorrow - would you like to come?"

"I don't know yet. We'll see how I feel when I get up if you don't mind", answered Merla. Merla got used to having a lie-in and then sauntering down to the shops on Saturday so she felt getting up to go to church which was nearly a whole day affair, would mean she would have lost a day of rest. She was no longer a Seventh Day Adventist - more a Baptist or a Methodist now, with church service on a Sunday. She was aware the church was a place where the whole community thanked God, prayed, and worshipped. However, it was also a social gathering place where people judged, gossiped and she was not ready for any questions from nosy busybodies. She thought they were insular and never left where they were born, grew up; let alone going to another town or for that matter going abroad. Merla had moved on and her experience meant she had nothing in common with these people. If she went to church, she would be going simply to please Aunt Bess and Uncle Harry and to set a good example to Eddie, Gloria, and Jenny. She had no problem with God as she really believed in Him and the church, but she had problems with the people who went every week. Whenever she thought of them she remembered the song, "By his Deeds" by Beris Hammond, which she thought summed up some Christians, especially in the country area. The gossip-mongers already knew she was visiting but she didn't want to give them the opportunity to ask her anything.

The next morning she decided not to go to church, but dressed Jenny and combed her hair, as she didn't want to upset the routine of Aunt Bess and the family. The family was conservative in their attire. Uncle Harry wore his suit and tie, finishing off with his hat and immaculately shined shoes. Aunt Bess wore the hat Merla brought for her and Gloria and Eddie were smartly dressed, although less formal and being much more aware of style than the adults. After they left, Merla went back to relax in bed. The dinner already cooked permitted her to rest and reflect on what she would be doing when she returned home with Jenny.

They seemed to be at church for ages Merla thought. Memories flooded back to her. Merla remembered when she was young how bored and hot she was, with large fans, merely circulating hot air, working overtime but seemingly no breeze coming from them; trying to keep awake in the heat and listening to the service with an adult nudging her if she nodded off. By the time the first part of the service broke for the children to go into the Sunday school classes, she was bored rigid. Her attention for the Sunday school lessons did not last for the length of time expected and it took a special child to concentrate on the Bible and God for that length of time. There were some good times however: children built up friendships and that kind of innocent and genuine friendship was hard to find as an adult. She hoped to replicate that kind of security she had as a child, whether it was aided by the church or if she did on her own. As she now thought she had everything in place for their new life, she was getting restless. Already she had started to look at her calendar counting down the days when they would be leaving. Now she could not wait to put her plans into action.

As it must be time for the family to return, Merla got up and started to reheat the already cooked meal and set the table. By 3.00 o'clock, they were home. So that's from 9.30am until 3.00pm! They spent the time discussing, exchanging news, gossiping, lunching, but the Bible and its teaching was paramount. One could not be knowledgeable about the Bible. This Book was dissected and discussed, and passages distributed to read and studied during the week; and it was expected that people came prepared for discussion, and display some knowledge and proof that this was done.

The family took off their Sunday best and prepared for dinner. Merla realised they were hungry and tired so she put all the food in serving dishes on the table and they ate in almost silence after Uncle Harry graced the table. The day was a Holy day so they frowned upon idle chattering and noise. It's was a day of reading the Bible, prayer and reflection with reserved and gracious demeanour. Having nearly finished the meal, they discussed about what happened that week and what the forthcoming week would hold for them. Uncle Harry updated everyone about what was happening on the farm, describing those who hadn't turned up for work or those who turned up on the Friday to be paid. Merla reminded everyone she would be returning to the UK on Friday and how she hoped the coming week would play out. They then retired to their corners in the house: Aunt Bess and Uncle Harry on the veranda, she with her Bible and him with his contemplative quiet persona. Eddie and Gloria went into their rooms to chill and/or to catch up on homework that needed finishing off. Merla read to Jenny and then relaxed on the lounge settee.

It wasn't long before night had engulfed the entire place. It was very dark outside although it was only just 7.00pm. That was another of the peculiar thing for Merla about the country. The towns had street lights but the country had no street lights to lighten the surrounding areas and one had to rely on lights from houses to direct the eyes. The darkness and animal noise, be it dogs barking spontaneously, or the crickets in the garden, added to the eeriness of the place. She prepared herself and Jenny for bed and the darkness outside helped Jenny to go to sleep as soon as her head touched the pillow. Merla took "The Pearl" to bed and quickly became engrossed in the book. She couldn't put it down although she was now tired and wanted to sleep. The book was easy to read, and enthralling, as it was readable on several levels, so she wondered whether other hidden messages had eluded her.

Sunday morning meant everyone rose relatively late. What a joy, no school, no church, no work! After breakfast, the phone rang and it was Pastor Morris. He heard Merla was visiting so he wanted to come and see her. Although slightly irritated, Merla agreed to see him, as she knew it was part of country life to 'pay respect'. The morning seemed to be dragging on so she passed the time colouring in a book with Jenny. This was very therapeutic for her as it filled her time and she didn't have to concentrate on anything.

"Miss Merla!" Pastor Morris announced.

"Hello Pastor Morris", she said opening the security grille door. "How are you keeping? Do you want a cold drink?" She asked as beads of sweat were running down his forehead.

He was more interested in how she was doing, so he didn't respond to the question of a cold drink.

"I'm doing well; can't complain. I have been truly blessed by the Good Lord since I left to go abroad. I really can't grumble", said Merla.

Responding, Pastor Morris said, "Yes, He is definitely alive and He never fails us".

Aunt Bess joined in the conversation on the veranda.

"Yes, He never fails us. Our Father is a loving and forgiving Lord. Even when we think He is not there, caring for us, He is".

Merla had forgotten whether she had an answer to the question about the cold drink, so she asked him again.

"Yes please. A glass of ice water please".

Quickly Merla excused herself to fetch the iced water.

She thought the conversation was already finished, but it had just begun with him and Aunt Bess.

"If only I could excuse myself and go and read my book. I have really finished with niceties and updates. Nothing more to say, but how do I excuse myself?" she thought.

"So Merla, how is the Mother Country?"

"It takes some getting used to. When I first arrived, I nearly got on the next flight back. I was really miserable and lonely. I hated the changeable cold weather. Some people can be very fickle and some quite unfriendly. Some very kind and friendly and their way of doing things is so different to this country but once I got used to these niggling problems, it became easier and soon I began to wonder, why don't all countries operate the same way. Practice such as queuing and the general discipline plus the overall structure and organisation. Don't get me wrong, you have to work hard, but if you lose your job, there is a safety net. You don't have to be on the street begging. There are some great qualities with the country. The obvious one is the NHS. So much we take for granted with our health. The education system is not the best but it is mainly the school; again, if you are in the right area, your child can go to a very good school. Some white children take their education for granted, as it's free. Blacks and immigrants have to work much harder than their fellow-workers to get a good job, but at least they have the opportunity. Hope for a brighter future is possible. The politicians are more accountable for their actions. Well at least that is what I observed".

Merla thought she was getting too political. She was on the verge of cursing off the Island's government but she retreated by closing the discussion with a feeble conclusion. "I suppose we as human beings accept most situations and it's not always as bad as we think".

She thought she needed to pay Jenny attention, so she excused herself.

"Thanks for coming to see us and please give my regards to your dear wife".

Merla retreated into the room with Jenny where they were now looking out of the window. She could not stop looking at the panoramic view outside. In the foreground, there was an assortment of bougainvillea plants: lilac, orange, pink, white, and yellow - all fully established and appear to have *planted* themselves as they were arranged in an ad hoc manner. Interspersed between these were the showy pink and white hibiscus, which had attracted butterflies and bumblebees onto their stamen. Although she was familiar with these plants, it never failed to fill her with wonder as to how such delicate flowering plants such as the hibiscus or the bougainvillea could withstand such heat without wilting or dying. Further, on past the lawn, in the middle ground, Uncle Harry had planted peas, lemon, and grapefruit, orange and in the background, there were bananas shoots, coconut, mango, and breadfruit and ackee trees. In the background, various green leaves were just about visible. She had surmised they were probably yam, potatoes, or pumpkin. No wonder they were self-sufficient and hardly needed to buy any food from the supermarkets! She heard when Pastor Morris said goodbye so she re-emerged onto the veranda.

"A very nice man of God," said Aunt Bess.

"And so he should be - he's a preacher!"

"Girl, don't let that fool you; some of these preachers are worse than the criminals out here. They are a bunch of thieves. When the poor people give them weekly tithes, this goes into their pockets and they don't do what they say they are going to do with the money. Every now and again, they are caught and there is a bit of scandal and then people forget and it's back to normal. They are not all good. When they are sitting pompously in the rostrum, they remind me of a rogue's gallery", said Aunt Bess.

"But you sound very cynical". "Is corruption that widespread in the churches? When they are found guilty, are these people prosecuted?"

"Usually they get away with it when they know people in high places. Money is the root of all evil. You know we are simple people; we just mind our own business and watch the world go by. Of course, we hear what's going on - we don't need to read any newspaper".

The days sped by quickly but she was determined to go to the beach at least once before leaving, so on Wednesday she and Aunt Bess with Jenny went to the seaside. As she lay on the white sand, almost as fine and hot as baked flour, protected only by a towel, she reflected on what a beautiful country she was leaving.

As far as the eyes could see, cobalt blue met ultramarine blue across the horizon. How wonderful and peaceful the beach was with most bathers at work or the holidaymakers had not yet woke up. They were nearly the only ones occupying the beach.

By Thursday, Merla packed the suitcase. Tomorrow she would be leaving. Most of the things she had brought with her she would leave as they were presents and toiletries, so she only packed the essentials, plus a few things for Jenny as she was determined to use just one suitcase, especially now she had a three year old with her. Her shopping comprised of all the things she couldn't get in the UK. Even if she could get these in the UK, they would not be as fresh and they would be so much more expensive. Items bought included food seasoning, tinned ackee, guava jelly, peppercorn, pimento seeds, and buns. In addition, she couldn't return without a couple bottles of rum as this was a fraction of the cost, but these would be kept for cake baking and punches.

Friday came quickly when it was time for Merla to return to the UK with Jenny. They had already said goodbye to Uncle Harry, Eddie, and Gloria who had left for work and school. Both mother and daughter were ready an hour before the taxi she ordered arrived. By now, the tension of waiting had now built up to a crescendo. Tears rolled down Aunt Bess and Merla's face. Jenny looked on and before long, she too had now mirrored the adults crying. They realised this weeping wasn't helping Jenny so they dried their eyes and composed themselves.

"I promise you that Jenny and I will visit you during the summer holidays. It won't be long before you'll be seeing us again. I just want you to know I love you and thank you for all your help. I will ring you as soon as we arrive home. Take good care of yourself", said Merla.

"I know you are doing this for the best. Look after yourself and Jenny. Remember if things don't work out, we are here......."

The goodbye was so sad Merla was relieved when the taxi drove off. She could now compose herself and concentrate on Jenny. At the airport, people were alighting from taxis, buses, and cars. Everybody seems to be flying out on the same day as her. Jenny was getting grizzly, as she probably felt she was in a strange situation and pinning for her Aunt Bess and her normal environment. The long wait through Customs didn't help the situation. They were slow in processing the passport and baggage, which irritated Merla. Just as well she was early. After the tension of the family goodbye and customs, Merla was now completely chilled-out and took advantage of focussing on Jenny.

The time spent going through customs meant it wasn't long before passengers were on board and the plane was taking off. Luckily for Merla, Jenny was exhausted and it didn't take her long to fall asleep although it was late afternoon. They spent most of the journey sleeping and just as well, as they would travel through the night and this meant the journey would appear relatively shorter. As she reclined in the chair, she looked down at Jenny and reflected on how she was now responsible for another human being.

"I am going to try my hardest and do my best for this little person". "No one is going to get between us", she thought.

The plane landed on time. The added little person by her side, a suitcase, and her handbag reminded her of the adult responsibility she now had. She was concerned but the taxi she ordered was on time when they got out of the airport. It was a Saturday so the taxis were busy doing other jobs so there were fewer available. She was glad she ordered it from her local taxi company before she left, as she would have had to wait for ages, and some do not want to drive that far from the airport to her home as they earned more for more frequent, shorter journeys.

CHAPTER 2

Jenny entered her new abode very tentatively. Although she couldn't verbalise what she was feeling, Merla realised everything was strange for her: the houses, the people, the environment, the weather. She looked cold and frightened. Her mother tried to reassure her with lots of cuddles, and kisses. The plane landed in the morning but by the time they got home, both felt extremely tired. It was going to be a lazy Saturday as both needed to recover from the long journey. In fact, Sunday would also be an easy day as Merla had booked off another two weeks to be with Jenny and sort out her affairs. She was sensitive to Jenny missing Aunt Bess and the only environment she ever knew.

"I need to try my hardest to make her as comfortable and secure as possible, so tomorrow we are going to the park which is just down the road", Merla thought to herself.

The suitcase could be unpacked tomorrow. After making a quick call to Aunt Bess to say they had arrived safely, the two had an early night and slept peacefully in Merla's bedroom. They were so tired, that they didn't wake up until 9.00am. This was late for Merla who was used to getting up early, even at weekends when she could have a lie-in. The flat was a converted post-war house divided into two flats with bay windows, two bedrooms, kitchen, bathroom, and living room. Merla bought the ground floor flat when she got a generous unexpected bonus that year when the company did well. After all, the employees had worked incredibly hard that year so in a way it was not a surprise at all, but it was truly wonderful to have received so much to be able to pay the deposit on a flat; 'a testament to Merla's hard work'.

This was her first and only job since she arrived in the country but Merla grasped legal matters quickly and she liked the topic.

She was saving for a deposit as soon as she started to work there, but this bonus was like a windfall and it accelerated the flat purchase. As an immigrant, Merla was aware that it was better to buy as some property owners didn't want to rent to black tenants. To analyse Merla she had to invite you into her world. Few people got close enough for her to disclose to them her plans. She had few friends but knew several people. She could be friendly, she but was a private person. She was a stoic driven person who had to grow up real fast, especially since having Jenny. Her innocence and trust in people had prematurely diminished, so trusting people was a challenge for her.

"Today I am going to introduce you to Mrs Green, my surrogate mother". Merla said to Jenny, who just looked at her uncomprehendingly but answered with a smile.

Mrs Green or rather Mrs G to Merla lived a few houses from Merla. They met when Merla moved into the flat. She was the first person to knock on Merla's door and offered her a cup of tea and cake when she moved in. Mrs G was warm and friendly; Merla felt relaxed with her although there was an age gap. It wasn't long before a 'mother'/'daughter' relationship developed. Mrs Green was a West Indian nurse arriving in the country from the West Indies in the '60s. She was one of the pioneering immigrants who took the opportunity and migrated to the mother country England, to study nursing. On completing the nursing course, she worked in a London hospital where she met her husband, who was working as an electrician in the hospital where she worked. Her beloved husband Sidney died prematurely of prostate cancer at the age of 55. His demise made her reflect on life and when she had a health scare she decided to retire early especially now their children, Nathan and Natalie, had flown the nest. Mrs G was the only person Merla told about her plan to get her daughter and bring her up single-handedly. In fact, Mrs G encouraged her by telling her she would be able to help with the childcare as she was at home. Mrs G was a God-fearing woman who attended church every Sunday. Apart from that, she was a homely, pleasant person. She was the type of person whose personality and intelligence shone through once you got to know her. They were there for each other and she was a very important person to Merla. This was a reciprocal relationship. Merla called in on her at least twice a week on her way home from work to make sure she was fine. They chatted about *back home*, work, about church, about people, about politics, you name it, - they really could chat. Although there was a big age gap, they shared the same values, ambitions and in many ways, they shared the same ideals. So many mothers and daughters have completely different ideas and the relationship is fraught with arguments, but for them, there was a connection. It may well be because they *chose* each other; friendship or family was not foisted on them. More importantly, they offered each other something, which was necessary in the other's life.

Mrs G's house was typically West Indian. There was a front room, adorned with doilies. The display cabinets housed beautiful unused Murano glasses and expensive bone china ornaments, probably purchased when she was working. The three-piece sofa, made from brown crushed velvet, and contrasting material, looked new as rarely had anyone sat in the front room. The multi-patterned carpet clashed with the rug, but it didn't really matter as these furnishings were bought to state signs of success through hard work and upward mobility. All these conspicuous adornments portrayed signs of a successful immigrant, who had now acquired the trappings of visual wealth.

Before Merla could prepare the breakfast, the phone rang and it was Mrs. G.

"Hi my lovely how was your trip?"

"Great - we just got up but we were coming to see you after your church service, if you are going to church that is".

"Well I am going to church but I will leave as soon after the service is finished. I will not wait around talking; I'll come and see you straight afterwards. Is that OK with you?" asked Mrs G.

"We'll be here waiting for you. The trip was fine but I won't keep you any longer, we'll talk more when you get here. OK? Speak to you soon."

Merla continued making breakfast and she and Jenny ate together in their dressing gowns. Jenny still seemed bewildered so Merla spoke to her as she placed the breakfast on the table. In her conversation with Jenny, she reassured her that she would be talking to Aunty B when they woke up, as there was a time difference. Again, it was porridge, but this time it was Scotch porridge oats, as that was what was available in the cupboard. Jenny ate but she wasn't that keen on it, or it could be the taste was new to her. Their hunger forced them to be less discriminating. This *getting to know you* was difficult for them both but even more so for Jenny as she, being a 3 year old couldn't verbalise how she was really feeling. Merla was aware of this so after breakfast, they went into Jenny's bedroom and went through the new toys and clothes she had bought her. Just by reading books, coupled with a natural instinct, Merla had endeavoured to make Jenny's bedroom as stimulating as possible, decorating the room with vibrant colours of yellow, green, and orange. Toys burst out of the now filled toy boxes, and stacked on the bookshelves were books such as "The Jolly Postman", "The Tiger who came to Tea", "Mog The Forgetful Cat", "Each Peach Pear Plum" and all the other nursery rhyme books Merla could find in the bookshop. Being an inexperienced mother, and not being sure how big a three year old ought to be, she bought a few different clothes sizes for Jenny. Smartly she kept the receipts and tags remained on the clothes in case they had to be returned to the shop. She helped Jenny with the trying on of her new clothes and ensured the ones she put on were warm, as although it wasn't yet winter, Jenny hadn't yet acclimatised to the colder temperature. These activities diverted Jenny's attention and took away any distress she may be feeling; a relief for Merla who was still learning about her child's feelings and behaviour. How she was handling the situation was dependent purely on motherly love and instinct.

The doorbell rang. Sure enough, it was Mrs Green. They greeted each other with enthusiastic hugs and kisses.

"So good to see you; I really missed you! You know she is the spitting image of you. I mean I don't know what her dad looks like, but I can see you in her and she has grown since I saw her photograph. Little Merla!" Mrs Green stooped to pick up Jenny but she wasn't having any of that. Jenny resisted her and went straight to her mother.

"Understandable", said Mrs G. "She's seen enough new faces and places in such a short space of time, I'd be the same".

"She'll change once she gets used to you", Merla said reassuringly. "I felt like a stranger when I saw her but little by little, she's warming to me. Do you want a cup of tea? Sorry, I don't have any food in the cupboard but we are going to the shops tomorrow to stock up on what we need".

"Girl, I didn't expect food; in fact I cooked some dinner for all of us. Want to come over later?"

"Thanks so much. I'm going to call Aunt Bess and let Jenny hear her and the family's voices, then I'm going to take her to the park to let her run around and introduce her to things like a swing. Then we'll pass by you. Is that OK with you?"

"Of course. We can go through what you want me to do for you when you go back to work. I know you said you have two weeks but the time is going to fly by so quickly".

Without stopping to take breath, the questions poured out of Mrs G's mouth. "So what was the place like? Has it changed and what did they say when you told them you were going to take Jenny with you?"

Merla didn't know where to start with the volley of questions so calmly she said. "Let's start with Jenny. When I told Aunt Bess, I felt she was upset but I think she realised it was inevitable. Her demeanour was quiet and at times sad, but as the week progressed, I think she accepted the situation. As to Uncle Harry, in his own reserved fashion, I still don't know how he really felt about this. He just said something to the effect '*Well you should know best*'. He is so placid; you really want to shake him sometimes! I think that's why Aunt Bess has had to take charge and be so hands-on in all the family affairs and approached everything with such passion and confidence. To be honest I was concerned as to their reaction, but was more worried how Jenny would feel, leaving them as she's only known that family and I was conscious the move may have had serious consequences on her. Now I have done it, I am so relieved I have taken that step".

Remembering the first question Merla answered, "Oh, the place has changed in many ways. In another way, nothing has changed. As usual, the poor people have to eke out a living here and there. They are so resourceful; I don't know how they do it. There is a lot of uncertainty about the future especially for the young people. What is different is it's even harder to get out of that poverty and leave the country. Young girls don't even finish school, they are getting pregnant as the boys refuse to wear condoms. Another issue that is happening that people don't talk about as its taboo and shameful, both to the victim and the area, is under-age sex, which we would classify as rape. This is sometimes hushed up by the family, who live in the community and dread the disgrace this would bring on them, so they pretend it's a *happy expectation*. Some of the girls get pregnant because they are so desperate for love and attention, the boys sweet-talk them, and before long, they are pregnant. I have really thought about it - a lot of it has to do with poverty, boredom, naivety, low self-esteem and the feeling of *'what's the point?'* A little like what happened to me, but they seem to be getting younger and younger! No recreational facilities such as youth centres, netball, football, or art clubs are available for young people at the weekends or in the evenings. I love our culture and the music but the only thing they seem to have to offer the youngsters is dance hall music blaring all over the area. It's quite depressing really. It's not that they don't have any ambition, a lot of them aspire for a better life, but the government has no desire to change the status quo. All they do is have meetings. Nothing comes out of these meetings. They only think about themselves. I get so angry when I think how these so-called politicians don't care. They couldn't give a damn about the poor people as long as they are all right and being paid for having meetings. It's very much a 'I'm alright Jack' mind-set. Every time I think about these politicians, from the local government to the people supposedly running the country I get so annoyed, as they are a selfish bunch of ass-holes. Excuse my language, but they are so awful, my language doesn't convey how awful and uncaring they are.

"The churches are still active helping where they can, but they are also helping themselves. Poor people are expected to give, what I consider, a large part of what they earn in tithe. Now and again someone spills the beans as to what has happened to the money, probably because the whistle-blower didn't get his fair share. Can you wonder why I am so sceptical about these churches sometimes, where there is no accountability or proper bookkeeping?"

I did go to the beach one day, not because I necessarily wanted to, but you can't visit the country and not go to the beach. That would be outrageous!"

Bored with the adults' conversation, Jenny broke free and went into her room to play with her new toys.

Mrs Green now got up to leave. "We'll talk more later. Bye, bye Jenny!"

Mother and daughter were now ready to explore the park. The park was a place where Merla never ventured before. Walking alone aimlessly in the park was a luxury. She thought only people with children or those who had lots of time on their hands used the park.

It was divided into grass areas, a children's play area, walkways, cycling pathways, evergreen trees of varying sizes and shapes and resplendent with colourful flowerbeds. As they walked, Merla took the opportunity to explain everything she perceived may be educational or of interest to Jenny. Merla had no idea what she was doing or how she could interest a 3-year-old child, so she clumsily resorted to formal educational mode. For the trees they passed, she went into a complicated presentation about trees to a 3 year old. "Trees play a very important role in our lives in reducing erosion; they remove carbon dioxide from the atmosphere and store large quantities of carbon in their tissues. We use trees to make our chairs and tables. They provide a habitat for animals and plants." Just as she said that, a squirrel emerged from one of the hollow parts of a branch. This fascinated Jenny, as she had never seen a squirrel before. It was tame and came forward for food but they had nothing to give it so it scampered off. That was a little disappointing as Jenny's face had lit up when it approached them.

"Next time we'll bring some peanuts and bread for the squirrels and swans".

The playground was full of mothers and fathers as it was before Sunday lunch and that is something many families did on a Sunday. Some of the rides they had to wait patiently to get on but Jenny loved the swing and

Merla had difficulty getting her to try any other rides once she was on this. As she pushed her, the smile and laughter on her face was worth all the effort Merla had made to get her child. Merla sang nursery rhymes to elaborate the enjoyment on the swing. "A, B, C, D, E, F, G ...." She just started to appreciate what motherhood could be like.

As they walked, Merla took the opportunity to talk to Jenny but the conversation was very one-sided as Jenny could just about say a few words, like dog, cat, and bird and very short sentences.

After a couple of hours, they were getting hungry so Merla decided to go on to Mrs. Green's place.

"I'll have to ask Mrs G if she is where she ought to be, or if she was slow for her age." Merla thought to herself. She questioned her maternal ability, as typically she was not in full control of this situation, lacked maternal confidence, and wanted to *fix* what she perceived as imperfect.

Jenny watched television while Merla helped to set the table and put the food on the table.

Mrs Green served up the usual gastronomic aromatic delight, which comprised rice and peas and jerk chicken, washed down with home-made carrot juice, a favourite Sunday meal for the family.

"Do you think she's slow for her age?" Merla asked in a hushed voice so Jenny couldn't hear her.

"What do you mean?" asked Mrs. Green.

"Is she talking enough for her age?" whispered Merla.

"Although I've just met her, I think she is fine. You don't expect to converse already with her, do you? Remember she is only 3 years old and children are all different; they develop at different ages. Take for instance our children; Natalie was more advanced than Nathan was although she was younger. I never thought he would get out of nappies. What a lazy so-and-so he was?

There came a time, I thought the little devil was being spiteful. You can always get an idea how they are developing by the unspoken response you get when you speak to them. For example, do they understand what you say? If you're still not sure, when you take her to register with your doctor, have a word with her and tell her your concerns, but really you'll soon learn so I shouldn't worry."

Mrs G graced the table and they all tucked in, as everybody was hungry.

"I don't know how you manage to constantly make your chicken so tasty. I have seen you cook so many times, watch and copy the recipe but it never tastes as good."

"Girl when you've been cooking for as long as I have, with the amount of practice I've had, if I can't cook by now, I'll never be able to cook. However, thanks for the compliment; it's great to get feedback and I appreciate when people love my cooking. So I'll pick up Jenny from the nursery three days a week and keep her until you come home from work and the other two days I will keep her for you all day. Is that right?"

"Yes - I'll give you her food and drink." Awkwardly Merla asked, "I don't know what to suggest regarding payment, but how does £200 a month sounds to you? You know I would give more but I have to pay the nursery and until I work out expense, that's all I can afford at the moment. I hope that's OK with you?"

"You know I'm not doing it for the money."

"Of course I know, but you should be paid for what you are doing. I'm just happy you can help me. I'm so grateful to you as I know I won't have to worry about the care she will get from you. Thank you so much". Merla said while giving her a hug and kiss.

Apple pie and ice cream rounded off the meal. When they finished talking and it was time to leave, Merla told Mrs G she'd be sorting out the nursery, registering her with the doctor and all the other important things that needed to be sorted before work recommenced. Most importantly, she needed to spend time with Jenny so they got to know each other.

The week started with registering Jenny with the relevant authorities, and at the doctor and finding out about nurseries. She thought nothing ever ran as smoothly as she wished. The nursery she wanted, because of convenience for Mrs Green to pick up Jenny, was fully booked so she had to choose the nearest available, which would mean taking a bus. The next best thing was to put Jenny on the waiting list for her nearest and opt for the one that had a vacant space. She wished she had registered her before going to collect her. Not her first choice but as with everything, 'you don't always get what you want … well not immediately anyway'.

Time sped by quickly and before long, it was time for Merla to do a dummy run of their daily journey, as with the further journey, they had to leave earlier in the mornings. In addition, she took the opportunity to take Jenny into work to introduce her to her workmates and her boss. Jenny was not a surprise to her boss or colleagues, as she never hid Jenny from anyone. She took every opportunity to talk about her.

Her relationship with her boss was an easy, open and an amenable one as Merla was a professional, hard worker. At her appraisal, her boss told her they were pleased with her hard work and her ability to grasp somewhat complex information, with very little supervision. Her boss was however concerned as to how she would cope when Jenny was sick, when Merla had to work late, school holidays, etc; all the issues that would concern anyone, let alone a single parent having to cope alone. Merla reassured her boss Cyril that she had already planned for all the anticipated and unexpected problems and she would cope; as she always have done and will continue to do.

Cyril was a stocky built middle-aged man who was quietly-spoken, and was an extremely bright lawyer. Married with three grown-up children, he was a considerate boss who could spot baloney and a phoney a mile off. He admired commitment and hard work and had the ability to get the best from his workers. His workers loved and admired him so much; they would do anything for him. He reciprocated by being a loyal, faithful, and supportive boss. Her colleagues were cordial and Merla had no idea how they felt about her but on the face of it they were friendly and appeared pleasant most of the time. Racism was around but as far as she was concerned, it was the racists' problem. What she learnt very early in her working life was not to get involved in office gossip, not to care what people thought, but to gain respect through her hard work, with poise and integrity. She had a goal and her secret mantra was: *'It doesn't matter what happens to you in your life, it's how you deal with it'*.

A couple of days before returning to work Merla decided to get Jenny familiarised with the new schedule and so she took her to the nursery and stayed with her for the first day until late morning. It was difficult, not just for mother but daughter too, but she could see Jenny would settle as she was already been drawn to two of the children her age, who welcomed her into their little group.

Gingerly Jenny participated in group games and played with the unfamiliar toys littered on the floor. The next day Merla left her after half an hour and she stayed there until 3.00pm. Jenny was tired and struggled to stay awake until bedtime at 7.00pm. The time she went to bed was crucial, as Merla did not want her to go to sleep when she got home from nursery and then wake up during the night, as this would be a problem for her when she returned to work. Therefore, they talked after dinner and cuddled up on the sofa after the evening news. Soon she bathed her and after a couple of bedtime stories, Jenny fell fast asleep. The rest of the evening now belonged to Merla, not just to clear up but also to shower and watch whatever she wanted to watch on television, make telephone calls to friends or to continue reading that book she had started and kept hoping to finish before returning to work.

The back-to-work day came round quickly and on that day Merla rose extra early. She wanted to prove to everyone, including herself that she could manage. Clothes they would be wearing, were placed neatly across the chairs, bags packed, lunch bag packed and pushchair in place, all ready for their journey.

On day one, the bus stop line was extending past the shelter, but because of her early start, they were ahead in the queue. As the bus slowly crawled towards them, the door opened even slower, a grumpy-faced driver greeted them. She struggled with the pushchair on the bus but mastered collapsing it quickly within a week. That first day was unlike the dummy run, as she couldn't hang around the nursery hoping Jenny would settle down. She just kissed her and said she would see her later. Jenny reciprocated with a wave. Merla then went to catch her train to work. She was apprehensive about leaving Jenny but on getting to work, she was quickly immersed into her many tasks so this distracted her motherly instincts. At about twelve noon, she rang the nursery to find out if Jenny was OK. Hearing she was fine, helped her to relax about the situation. She then phoned Mrs Green to remind her about the pick-up at 3.00pm.

"Of course I haven't forgotten", she reassured Merla. Having had children already, this would be a piece of cake to Mrs G. Already she had in her mind how the week would pan out, with keeping Jenny in the afternoon, and the two days she has her, what she would be doing on those days. One day included taking her to the library, which had a large selection of children's books for her to read to her. One of the days, she hoped to take her to the park and then another day, maybe the zoo, which was a small local zoo, with questionably aged animals. At least Jenny would get an idea of what the animals looked like in the flesh. Already Mrs G had dug out the old videos of Sesame Street from the loft, ready for her on the days they didn't venture to the park. The same videos her children watched when they were young.

"Just as well I didn't get rid of the video recorder which I expect is now obsolete", she mumbled to herself.

It was a busy day for Merla, as she had to catch up with her boss what had happened during the past few weeks, reading her file notes, prioritising the urgent work, and generally cracking on with the work. Her desk was stacked with files, which had yellow stickers, and notes updating on what was done or what phone calls had come through in her absence. With her first day's schedule, she didn't have time to stop to have lunch and just asked one of her colleagues to buy her a sandwich when out. The first day was hard. Merla dashed down the stairs at the train station to catch her train home. Gone were the days when she could saunter home at whatever time she wanted, working late to avoid the rush hour. That had now gone and she did not want to get off to a bad start with Mrs G. In her briefcase were notes she would be looking over after putting Jenny to bed.

Jenny was pleased to see her mother, and Mrs. Green briefed Merla on what the nursery had said about Jenny's proper first day.

"The nursery said she was quiet to start with but went to play with the children she met on her first day. She had her lunch with the other children and rested in the afternoon. By the end of the day she was settled although a little tired from the day's activities".

That day Mrs G and Merla had only a cursory chat before waving goodbye. It wasn't long before everyone was now familiar with the schedule and things went smoothly. The weeks and months went by quickly and before they looked round, it was the end of October. The clocks went backwards which was a sign that winter was around the corner. Merla remembered this when she was first introduced to the phrase 'spring forward, fall backward'. The autumn, with its varying shades of oranges, browns, reds, and yellows, had always fascinated Merla from the first day of her introduction to autumn in the country, as this was an unusual experience for someone who was used to a tropical climate with only subtle seasonal changes. The Caribbean may have trees losing their leaves but it was not as noticeable. Verdant trees still dominated that landscape. Organising hers and Jenny's daily life was not an easy task and the shorter days, dark evenings left her feeling low sometimes. She spent her evenings doing chores and looking after her daughter. Having less time to develop any friendships or going out in the evenings, she opted for sporadic phone calls to the few people she knew, after putting Jenny to bed. Being a single mum meant she had already resigned to the fact that good men may judge her so she resigned to not bothering to make an effort to socialise. This was never going to be easy, especially as she was usually very tired after work anyway, but the long dark evenings certainly did not help.

Although she was aware that nothing could progress before the next 2 years anyway, Merla spent the long dark evenings researching what she needed to do to move forward now she has her child with her. She wanted to do so much to improve their lives. She was ambitious, as ultimately she wanted to earn enough to live a comfortable life and to give her child the best possible future. There was also a bit of wanting to make her family proud of her, and compensating for her 'mistake'. As she had done in the past with the course, she researched how and what she needed to do to move forward in her career. Her employers and particularly her boss would be crucial in this next phase.

The daily routine became easier and winter was now here. Jenny's first winter was disappointing in a way for her mother as Merla was looking forward to introducing her to snow, but there was no snow that year; only very cold and windy days and nights. Trees bared their branches, grass with a thin film of frost and a gossamer of cobwebs, abandoned by their inhabitants, now adorned the outside areas. Jenny had a couple of colds and runny nose but nothing serious that winter. She was talking a lot more since she arrived at nursery school. Interacting with other children and adults at the nursery must have helped her speech. Invitations for friends' birthday parties became the norm for Jenny.

One evening collecting her, Mrs Green said to Merla in private. "Out of the blue you'd never guess what Jenny asked me today?" "Where's my dad?"

"I was not completely shocked but she caught me off-guard so I said to her "Why did you ask that my love?"

"Anne and Linda have dads", she replied.

"I told her I would find out and either I or you would get back to her with an answer".

"You know I knew this would happen but didn't expect she would ask so soon. I was hoping I could control when I told her. I hope that when she got older, but she needs to know sooner than I thought. I will have a think about it and speak to her later when we are reading books. I hope that I am doing the right thing by explaining to her when we are reading. That time seems to be the best time for getting her complete attention whilst she feels secure with me hugging her in her warm bed. I will probably ring you later to get your advice when I have it clear in my head how I will explain this to her".

"Keep it light and short; children that age can't comprehend or take in too much explanation," Mrs Green added. "Speak later".

Merla got home and while she sorted out the dinner and her chores, she pondered as to the exact words she would use to eradicate any negative thoughts her daughter may be carrying about not having a dad. Children want to belong to a group; they want to blend in with others so it wasn't surprising. After dinner and bath time it was time for bed. Merla just had time to ring Mrs G. to tell her what she was going to say at bedtime reading.

In bed, they read stories and halfway through this, Merla said to Jenny. "You know mummy loves you dearly and she will do anything for you. I absolutely adore you. Nanny G told me you asked why haven't you got a dad like your friends? Some of your friends will have dads, some wont. You see darling your father and I were both young. We were young, stupid and in love. We didn't think things through and it wasn't long before you came along. We couldn't get along and we agreed it was best to go our separate ways and Aunt Bess and Uncle Harry were happy to love and care for us both. Are you happy? Do you love mummy?" She hoped her answer was reassuring and comforting to Jenny and there would be no more difficult questions about the subject.

Jenny nodded a "yes".

The story reading continued and after finishing they hugged each other and with a kiss, Merla said "Goodnight, sweet dreams".

With a sign of relief, she hoped the answer eased any uncertainties the 3-year old may have had and Jenny never asked about her dad again.

Spring was now obviously here with its vibrant yellow daffodils and tulips peeping through the sodden ground, mixed with the bluebells vying for attention. Walking through the local park, Merla pointed out to Jenny the white cherry blossom and pink magnolia trees lining both sides of the pathways. They had now established a routine, where in the mornings Merla dropped off and collected Jenny in the evenings from Mrs G, and at weekends Merla did the housework: cooking, cleaning and preparing for the following week. She more than proved to her boss that she could cope with the extra responsibility. Her workload was unaffected as she brought work home and after sorting out Jenny, she would finish off whatever he requested of her. The next day she would nonchalantly present the answer or finish off anything her boss had requested from her the previous day. Only Cyril really knew how hard she worked with limited supervision.

CHAPTER 3

Two years sped by quickly and Jenny was now 5 years old. Merla had reserved a place for Jenny in the local primary school, which was closer than the nursery, so the journey was less arduous. It now meant Mrs Green was only going to look after Jenny after school and during the holidays. Merla bought the uniform and all the necessary add-ons such as lunch box, PE kit, and coat for the new school. On trying these on, Merla got emotional as she realised her daughter was getting big before her eyes.

The first week at new school was relatively easy, as Jenny had eased smoothly into the whole day schedule. She did find the structured work such as drawing, singing, reading and writing very tiring. When Mrs Green collected her from school, she tried to keep her awake with conversation, drawing, and watching the "Sesame Street" videos.

By the 2nd year at primary school, life was easier for everybody. Jenny no longer felt as tired by the afternoon but as soon as her mother came for her, she was ready to go home. One of the challenges for a parent with an only child was constantly being concerned that, without playmates, the child would be bored or watch too much television but Merla tried her hardest to keep her daughter stimulated when they got home.

Life was settling down for them both. Merla introduced the small number of friends she had to Jenny by inviting them round for coffee, drinks, and sometimes a light meals. Granted this was not as often as she would have liked as she continued to be very busy with work and housework.

One Saturday evening Merla invited her best friend, Ruth and her husband for dinner. Ruth was a bubbly, vivacious young nurse, whom Merla had met through a mutual friend. Their similar outlook and values made the relationship easy, amiable, and pleasant. Ruth was a couple of years older than her friend, who was now 23, but this made no difference as Merla was older in her attitude. Ruth married her *Mr Right* a year ago, after many broken relationships. Merla often wondered how she was able to stay so bubbly and upbeat after experiencing such hurt from former boyfriends. She thought Ruth was a lousy judge of character and felt she trusted too easily, but she never gave up. Being a nurse may have had a bearing on her compassion and not giving up but Ruth's belief system was very straightforward: if she did good, trusted people and could see the good in people, those qualities would override the negatives ultimately. Here lies a mixture of her spiritual and her Biblical beliefs: good always triumphs over evil. Merla found Ruth sometimes too good to be true but that was her character.

After qualifying as a nurse, Ruth worked in various hospitals and saw her job as a vocation. She loved people and as she saw death often in her job, she felt every day was a bonus and should be lived to the fullest, in peace and harmony. Her religious conviction and upbringing helped her to practise this belief in her daily life. Of course, this was not reality and her principles meant she was often in for a rude awakening. However, she never gave up on the human race. She met her husband, Monty when he was in hospital, having his appendix removed. Their mutual attraction was immediate. Ruth even joked to Monty that she knew about his stomach before she saw his face. Monty, a telephone engineer, was also a regular churchgoer. He was a softly spoken, laid-back individual who came along at the right time for Ruth and brought peace and stability into her life. That evening, Ruth confided to Merla:

"We're considering starting a family".

"Why *considering?*" asked Merla.

"We need a bigger place and need to sort this as if I stop working immediately, we won't be able to get enough extra mortgage for a bigger house. Starting a family also means I won't be able to work as regularly as I am now and I would only be able to work weekends, so you can see my dilemma. Not that my nursing salary goes very far but we need two incomes".

Monty smiled and added, "I told her not to worry, but you women...... It's never going to be a right time."

"I don't see this as a dilemma. Monty is right - unless you're rich, there is never going to be a right time, but you two have to decide", Merla added.

Ruth quipped, "Anyway, what are you doing about your love-life now you have Jenny with you and you are both settled"?

"Nothing...I am trying to sort out, not just my future, but hers too. It's not going to be easy. I can't allow anyone or anything to get in my way, as I have a plan and I cannot afford to have anyone complicating my life".

"Your problem is you have to learn to trust, let go and allow positive energy to flow into your life. You have to let things go. By opening the door of your heart, the wind of change will permit good energy to flow through your life. You, as much as anybody in the entire universe, deserve love and affection, and as the old Native American proverb goes: "The soul would have no rainbow if the eyes had no tears ......" We'll have to sort you out if you won't do it yourself my dear. Don't forget God is in all this so I'll pray that He will lead you to the right person or the right person will come to you." We are going to love you and leave you as I have to work tomorrow morning".

Jenny was fast asleep and Merla retired to bed, thinking about what Ruth had said to her. She recalled a poem written by Langston Hughes:

> *"Hold fast to dreams, for if dreams die*
> *Life is a broken-winged bird that cannot fly.*
> *Hold fast to dreams, for when dreams go*
> *Life is a barren field, Frozen with snow."*

That poem, together with Ruth's pep talk, resonated with Merla as she desperately tried to sleep. As she lay in bed, half asleep, she dreamt of finding the right partner. What would she want in her ideal man?

"Should it be financial security? Or looks? Humour? Should it be someone who was very aware of health and well-being? Should it be someone who took charge of her welfare and her life?" These questions floated round her head as she lay down but eventually she fell asleep. The evenings were now getting darker and shorter. This did not however deter Merla from looking at her plans. She also prepared herself for the next one-to-one with Cyril. As she had done in the past with the course, Merla realised she needed to talk to him to get his approval and to network with her co-workers, who were on a similar training programme. Cyril was therefore crucial in this next phase. Working as a legal executive was not an easy route to becoming a lawyer, but as she was already within a law firm that provided legal executive staff with an excellent opportunity to further their careers, she was able to put into practice some of the skills already acquired such as drafting and legal research. She heard about a colleague who was halfway through her course, so she arranged to take her to lunch to discuss this further. Without beating about the bush, Merla told her the reason for her call. Was she available for lunch and if so, could she spare a lunch break with her, to tell her how to proceed?

Sandra, her work colleague, a tall, 30-something, agreed to meet for lunch on the Thursday of that week. To Merla's amazement, Sandra brought with her a thick folder outlining how she worked. She explained how it was possible to apply credit of up to a maximum period of six months. Merla on the other hand, had a new empty notepad, with a few questions she was going to ask Sandra. They were not strictly strangers as they passed each other in the corridor and acknowledged with a smile as they hastily made their way through the long corridors with files under their arms.

The lunch meeting went well: they both gelled as there was mutual respect and understanding; neither felt threatened or out to prove anything. Sandra reminisced about how she felt when she started, so that was very supportive. Merla was grateful and Sandra sealed their parting with a hug, suggesting that if she needed any help, to email or call her and she would try her best to help.

Elated with the positive response from Sandra, she took her daughter out for a Friday evening fish and chips meal. She realised Jenny did not understand what she was saying to her, but it didn't matter as she was excited and needed to tell someone.

That weekend both mother and daughter had a relatively easy time as Merla had already prepared herself for the meeting with Cyril. He is fully aware of her intentions, as she had already broached the subject with him and it was his suggestion that they talked about it at the next meeting. The firm helped some who displayed the ability to progress towards becoming trainee solicitors. They also had to show not only potential, but ambition and tenacity. Cyril was familiar with the process.

The meeting lasted longer than usual as Merla came prepared, outlining to Cyril the type of research work she had undertaken for the company, and going through the experience she had already gained. Both were aware that her work ethics played a big part in determining whether she would qualify for a training contract. The meeting ended with Cyril promising to complete the necessary forms to change her contract from a legal executive to a trainee solicitor, starting as soon as the relevant departments had processed the papers.

This good news was still undisclosed to her co-workers but her steps were sprightly and her demeanour for the rest of the day was one full of confidence. Excitedly she told Mrs Green the good news about how the meeting had gone. Jenny did not understand the reason for the excitement but she relished her mother's happiness by responding with continuous laughter and playfulness. Feelings of enthusiasm permeated Merla's conversations.

That evening after putting Jenny to bed, she called a couple of her friends, including Ruth. Without giving her reason to answer in the negative, Ruth told her she was having a barbecue to celebrate the good news.

"A barbecue in winter? Steady on girl, let me get the new contract first".

"OK a dinner then. When are you going to get this?" retorted Ruth.

Without thinking too much about it, Merla said, "I expect within the next

3 weeks".

"Let me know as soon as possible so I can plan things".

"OK, will do".

Time flew so quickly and it was not long before Merla had received her new contract. Cyril was very happy for her and gave her a hug. She thanked him, went into the toilet, and shed a few tears. Tears of joy as she realised how she had come a long way in a short time, after joining the company and working hard. She was sure Cyril had something to do with the speed in which she received her new contract.

That evening on telling Ruth, she did not take long to set up a date for the dinner. She was unaware but Ruth's intentions were not completely innocent as she intended inviting a couple of potential single men for Merla to meet.

The day came in the late autumn but the day was like summer. Jenny went to stay with Mrs Green who offered to keep her. Mrs Green was aware that Merla needed a break, to enjoy herself for a change. Mrs Green thought she needed some adult interaction outside of work.

Merla arrived with flowers and drinks in one hand and a striking orange leather handbag in the other. It could be because she had not been out for a long time but she had made an extra effort and looked elegant in a plain cream dress, black high heels shoes, and a black shawl for the chilly evening. Apart from Ruth and Monty, Ruth invited two other couples, and two single men. One was Raymond and the other Charles.

Raymond was a newly promoted Accounts Manager, and Charles an IT Engineer. As the weather was mild, the outside tables were laden with wine glasses, fruit, bread rolls and nibbles. Monty was in charge of the barbecue, although Ruth had already seasoned the jerk chicken and pork. The hosts insisted that their guests should enjoy the event and refused any help with the cooking. Merla was definitely not dressed for cooking any food. The penny dropped and Merla realised Ruth's intention as she mingled with the guests. The first prospective *suitor*, Raymond, had a warm smile, OK looking, could be in his 30s, although his demeanour was more serious. This could well be because he had a neat moustache, which helped to make him appear more sombre. Charles, on the other hand, was more friendly, also in his 30s, but more talkative and appeared a more down to earth approachable person. Both men were attractive in their own way. Merla had a good afternoon; she talked and laughed as she mingled with the guests. Charles was talkative and her conversations with him were easy but Merla wasn't sure if he was covering up his shyness by being so lively. It could be he was uncomfortable with silence or that he liked her but did not know how to ask her for a date so he talked around every subject. Raymond was a little more circumspect. He seemed to be looking at Merla but liking her from a distance. Both men were probably confused because Merla did not express any obvious feelings for either of them. Subconsciously she slightly preferred Raymond because he appeared more challenging, but in no way was she going to chase him, especially if he was going to play hard to get. Merla chasing a man was never going to happen. She still had old-fashioned values where the man was supposed to do the chasing. She had also been hurt before and was not going to let that happen again.

The next day Ruth called her to ask what she thought about each of them. Both women laughed aloud when Merla said: "You are one scheming devil - did I tell you I wanted a man!? Anyway, where did you find these men… never seen them before".

"Monty met Charles through his work and they struck up a friendship. Raymond attends our church and funnily enough, he was the one who contacted me this morning, asking more about you. He likes you a lot but wanted to see if you liked him as well."

"Well, well, you could have knocked me down with a feather," said Merla. "In no way did he indicate he liked me yesterday when we talked. In fact, at one point, I wondered why you bothered to invite him. Funnily enough because he was more of a challenge, I was more interested in how he was feeling. His reverse psychology worked as the more he was a bystander, the more I wanted to draw him into the conversation. Was he shy, not interested, boring, or scheming?" Eventually I thought to myself, "Well mister, you are a grown man, I am not going to force you into the conversation any more".

"Both men are fine people but to be honest, I don't know enough about Charles to give a character opinion. He appears to be a friendly, chatty person, and he is more of an open book. In a way, it's a good quality to have I suppose and since I have met him, I haven't seen anything negative in him. Raymond, on the other hand, is more serious, but not as forthcoming. Although only 29 years old, he is however a deep thinker, but when you get to know him, he is a lovely human being. He is religious but not dogmatic in his belief and as you can see, he never foists his religious belief on anyone yesterday. You wouldn't know he goes to church if I hadn't told you."

"What do you think, Ruth? Not sure about either of them", said Merla.

"Well, Charles hasn't contacted me to show an interest in you, so you're just left with Raymond," chuckled Ruth.

"I'm not talking about Charles. In fact, I'm glad Charles hasn't contacted you as I would have had to decline. I don't mind outgoing people, but he may be too over-powering for me. I couldn't deal with that type of personality all the time. It would drive me up the wall. It could be because he was nervous. On the other hand, I don't want someone who is so quiet that I am doing all the work. I certainly don't want a controlling chauvinist but also don't want to be the one who always have to initiate a conversation with a man".

"OK. Before we go any further, when you speak to Raymond, in the conversation mention Jenny; tell him a little about me i.e. my age nearly (24 going on 43!) and if he still shows an interest in me, give him my number. I will not be contacting him, let him if he is interested. I don't have to tell you Ruth, I am going to take this slowly so just go easy".

A week went by. Now and again Merla thought about Raymond. Although she was interested in dating someone and Raymond appeared to be the ideal person, she wanted a relationship that was stress-free with a man who understood her aims and ambition. She wanted someone who most of all got on with her daughter and she in turn liked him. Jenny's happiness was most important and even if she dated anyone, she would not be introducing that person to Jenny for a while. In any case, he hadn't phoned her, so she felt that Jenny might have put him off so she put him out of her mind.

In the middle of the second week, at about 7.30pm the phone rang. Merla thought it was one of her friends, who generally called after she had done all her evening chores.

"Good evening Merla. It's Raymond. You may not remember me but we met at Ruth's & Monty's barbecue just over a week ago" he said formally.

Not meaning to play hard to get, ambivalent or too keen, Merla said nonchalantly, "Of course I remember you. How are you?"

A pause developed and Raymond took a while to respond.

"I'm fine. I didn't get to talk to you on your own and just wondered if you fancied dinner with me this weekend. I hate rejection so please don't say 'no'".

Both laughed and Merla answered casually.

"That sounds like a good idea but I can't do this weekend as I already promised my daughter, Jenny, that I would be taking her up to London to the Dolls House Museum in Bethnal Green."

"That's OK, how about the following Saturday?"

"Let me come back to you as I have to arrange for a baby-sitter. What's your number?"

Raymond gave Merla his number and asked her tenderly, "I know we won't be meeting for nearly two weeks, so can I call you before then?"

"Of course you can but call me after 8.00pm".

The conversation was measured, but warm and full of unspoken expectations. After putting the receiver down, Merla had a smile on her face and was excited.

The next day, now and again her absorption in her work was interrupted with her thoughts about Raymond. She had not dated for ages and wondered what she was going to talk about when he called her. She wondered if her conversation might appear staid or boring when they meet. What could she talk about to make herself more interesting. In truth, she had not had a relationship since she broke up with Jenny's father.

Saturday came and with lunch in bags, Merla took Jenny to the Museum of Childhood in London. She wasn't sure how much Jenny would be taking in or indeed whether she cared much about dolls and dolls houses, but wanted her to experience at an early age the idea of visiting museums. So many children got bored and agitated when they visited museums, as they were not used to that form of interaction; so neither the parents nor the children end up enjoying the experience. Merla wanted to avoid that. As they walked, Merla tried to explain the different style of houses through the ages. Now and again, a quizzical look appeared on Jenny's face. Could a child that age really understand the difference between a Georgian and Victorian dolls house? It did not matter, just time together was enough for them and mother and daughter enjoyed the day although, by the time they got the train, they were exhausted when they got home.

The week was busy but Raymond called her on the Sunday evening. They spoke about likes and dislikes, but being cautious and treading carefully by being light-hearted and avoiding, anything that may cause upset to the other.

By the next Friday, Merla was thinking about hairstyles and what she was going to wear tomorrow. It made her question her self-confidence now she was going on a date. Had she put on weight? Although she was slim, she started to find imaginary fat round her thighs and stomach. By Saturday afternoon, she was a nervous wreck. She left Jenny playing in her room and went for a quiet talk to God. Merla's prayer asked God to guide her, to help her to be wise and make the right decision; and if the man she was dating tonight was the right man for her and Jenny, to help them to develop the relationship and take it further. She thought to herself, imagine I haven't even met this guy properly and I am already talking about a relationship. "He could be awful so why am I running before I can walk?" she asked herself.

With Jenny now at Mrs G's house for the evening, she got ready and to steady her nerves, she sat down with a glass of wine, to wait for Raymond to arrive. With the taximeter still running, the doorbell rang and Merla greeted her date. As she was ready, they hopped into the cab.

"I don't mind where we go as I eat most things. I'll leave it up to you", she said.

"Glad you said that as I have booked a table for two at an Italian restaurant in town", said Raymond.

"The only Italian food I have ever eaten is spaghetti bolognese and lasagne so that's fine by me as I like both dishes. Plus I haven't had these for a long time".

When they arrived at the restaurant, they were ushered into a quiet corner, with candles as the only form of lighting. Raymond asked Merla what she wanted to eat and about her wine preference. She went for spaghetti bolognese and red wine. He ordered for himself vegetable lasagne and a bottle of red wine and water. While they waited for the food, they drank the wine and asked each other questions about themselves.

"So, tell me about yourself." Merla said as if interviewing Raymond. She might as well had finished her sentence with "….and why do you want to work with our company?"

"I am 29, an Accounts Manager, working in a fairly large corporation in the City. Recently I was promoted to Manager. You may be wondering why I am not married and settled with a few children. I only say this because most of my friends who are my age are married with children. Not that I am now looking to settle down I might add. It's just I have had a very active life, playing football, doing church activities and travelling. I would also like my partner to be a Christian and if not a Christian, be prepared to consider my faith as this is very important to me. I am quite happy and contented and live a fulfilled life, albeit without a partner. I lack patience which could be considered a negative trait but I am learning to change that".

"Give me an example of your lack of patience", Merla said.

"Well if someone complains to me about their manager being unreasonable as the manager keeps picking on them, I may ask them, 'So what are you doing differently to the other workers?' That person may say or imply, 'I am sometimes late, or I struggle to meet deadlines, but that shouldn't matter as I'm a hard worker'. The solution may not be that obvious of course. I may suggest that they are in control of the situation and should try to change their behaviour. I am very considerate when dealing with staff, as I would have already spoken to the manager before the interview with the complainant. Don't get me wrong, I know it's hard to change human behaviour but when something is so obvious, especially when told to a mediator, it's important to consider the solution. This is not a good example. I have had girlfriends, some serious, some casual, but for one reason or another, the relationship fizzled out because we just couldn't hack it. To be honest, I don't suffer fools gladly".

Raymond thought he had talked too much so then said, "So tell me about you".

"Well where do I start? I'm 24 and work as a legal executive in the City but recently I got a trainee solicitor's contract, which really excites me. My mother died when I was 5 years old but don't feel any sympathy for me as although I would have loved a natural mother, my Aunt Bess and Uncle Harry loved and cared for me like their own child.

To get this out of the way, Merla said, "I have a 7-year-old daughter, Jenny. Just before I was 17, I met this boy and thought we were in love. I was very naïve and a complete fool, as instead of studying my books, I became romantically involved and it wasn't long before I fell pregnant. In the country, teenagers are so foolish, and it happened to me. The same thing that happens to young girls all over the country. Imagine my first boyfriend and wallop – pregnant! My aunt and family were very disappointed with me but as always, they stood by me. Don't get me wrong, now I have my daughter, I love her to bits and wouldn't have it any other way but I feel sometimes, because I had a child early, people may be judging me as an easy, slack, tart. Nothing could be further from the truth: I am not a tart she said defensively and in fact, I haven't had a boyfriend since then. It's like a self-imposed punishment. Anyway, I took the opportunity my aunt and uncle gave me and came to this country on my own. I got a job in this solicitors' office, went to night school to improve my skills, and did a legal executive course. I feel as if I have something to prove to my family and myself, and to improve my life and Jenny's. It feels as if I have always been studying since leaving school. You could say my downside is I am very focussed and will not allow anything or anyone to get in my way of achieving my goal.

By now, the food had arrived. While they ate, they talked. They shared each other's history and to help the conversation along, they took it in turn to ask the other "If you were a …….. What would you be and why?

Raymond asked, "If you were an animal, what would you be?"

"An elephant, without a doubt: They are intelligent, decisive, confident, patient, and compassionate. They have an ability to work well as a group and cope well with adversity. I read something the other day that where leadership amongst other groups of animals is dependent on aggression, the elephant respects intelligence and problem solving in their leaders. I also love the way they care for their dying elephants with such dignity".

Raymond thought, "I am failing here as I told her I lacked patience".

To balance things and find the softer side of Raymond, Merla then asked him. "If you were a flower what would that be and why?"

"He thought about it and said. "That isn't a fair question as all flowers serve a purpose and are beautiful in their own way, but I have to go with the rose. I know it's soppy, but roses make perfumes, have health benefits such as rose hip syrup, ointments, they are useful in decorations, and they are symbolic: white rose: peace, red rose: love and I think they are linked to Christianity as well; very practical and also beautiful. Is your middle name Rose?"

"That question is such a corny chat up line! Wow! You do surprise me with your knowledge of the rose", said Merla.

By the time they finished eating, they were relaxed, and enjoying each other's company. Raymond filled her wine glass and asked her if she enjoyed the meal.

"How do you feel about us meeting up again?"

Merla smiled and hesitated with her response. "Would love to - I really enjoyed the meal and your company. What about you?"

"What do you think? You would by now know if I wasn't enjoying your company. I struggle with faking it; in fact, we would probably have eaten our food and be home by now! …… Of course I would love to see you again!" he said with a wide smile.

Raymond hailed a taxi and took her home. Merla tried to shake his hands to thank him, but he thanked her with a big hug. It was too late to collect Jenny so Merla spent the rest of the night resting by herself, dissecting the evening in her mind, wondering if she said anything wrong. Was she too open she wondered?

The next day, she picked up Jenny and explained to Mrs Green what Raymond was like, describing his characteristic, his appearance, and his behaviour. Although she described him, Mrs G didn't feel that there was much enthusiasm and emotion in her voice. Mrs G asked, "Well, do you like him?

"Yes, but at the moment, I can't get too excited; I am keeping my emotions and feelings well in check until I know him better. I really don't know him as yet".

"I suppose you are telling me to watch this space then? I understand", said Mrs. G.

The following week, the Trainee Solicitor's mindset kicked in, being even more conscientious and determined. In between her workload, she did think about Raymond and his evening phone calls helped her to realise he was still very interested in their relationship. They talked about current affairs, about life, about their work and colleagues but more and more it was about them and their relationship.

By Thursday, Merla got a call from Aunt Bess to say Uncle Harry was in hospital, as they were running tests to find out why he was losing weight. The news engulfed her. She phoned Aunt Bess every day to find out if they had yet received the result and asked if they wanted her to come over. Aunt Bess told her not to do anything yet as he looked fine and there could be several reasons for the weight loss. Merla reflected how she took life for granted but this news now brought home to her the fragility of life - one minute you are here and the next minute……

Over the next two weeks, Merla saw Raymond once although they spoke to each other more or less every evening. Their conversations were getting more relaxed and intimate. Merla thought about him a lot more and they would tell each other about their day, how they were feeling, and anyone who irked them that day; and about Uncle Harry's illness.

Being newly appointed as an Accounts Manager meant he had more responsibilities. What was challenging for him wasn't the work, but his colleagues. At 29, he was one of the youngest applicants for the promotion and had been with the company a shorter period than his colleagues. There was therefore a degree of resentment, built up since his appointment, as some of his colleagues felt they were more entitled to that job. It really didn't matter to Raymond what they felt about him as he knew in his heart that he worked hard, putting in the extra hours and achieving all the company's targets since joining and met all the criteria for the job. That jealousy was their problem and he felt with time they would accept the situation. Human are such inconsistent and unpredictable beings; their jealousy now superseded the camaraderie they once shared with Raymond.

Raymond was the eldest of three children, each spaced out precisely with a two-year gap. His sister was 27 and the youngest was a brother aged 25. Raymond had already bought his own flat when he was 26. His sister, a midwife, had now also purchased her own place so the biggest trouble was his brother, who thought his parents owed him something and would not budge from the parental dwelling. Raymond felt his brother was irresponsible and was not looking at changing his behaviour and thinking about the future. He was just having a good time and spending money like water. The number of arguments he had with his brother when he visited his parent's home was sapping his spirit. He was also angry with his parents for seemingly being complicit in this arrangement.

Both shared each other's angst, but Merla was still wondering why a woman had not snapped up Raymond long ago. Again, he reassured her he knew what he was looking for in a woman and most he had met, were incompatible with what he wanted. This made Merla felt special but paradoxically this also made her felt as if she was on trial. This had little to do with Raymond; it was more to do with how Merla was feeling about herself. Feelings of inadequacy and undeserving of happiness played a major part in how she felt about herself. A major question from Raymond, which was very important to him and hadn't yet been tackled, was how did Merla feel about God and attending church? Merla didn't mind going to church as she came from that background but didn't want to be forced. She wanted to make the decision to go to church herself. Having already had this out with Aunt Bess she didn't want to have to religiously go to church if she didn't want to. Aware of this, Raymond didn't come over as being dogmatic, but told Merla this aspect of his life was important to him. He left Merla to consider what he had said.

She shared her concerns about Uncle Harry. What should she do? Should she go and help Aunt Bess to deal with this new challenge or should she wait? Raymond could only comfort her by listening and empathising with the situation.

On Monday evening, she got the call she hadn't wanted. Uncle Harry had bowel cancer but they caught it early so the prognosis was good. Merla composed herself and asked Aunt Bess what she wanted her to do. Aunt Bess spoke to God and she was adamant He would save Harry. She would prefer any money Merla might use for fares for she and Jenny to cover hospital costs. Merla agreed but promised she would visit them as soon as possible. Immediately she phoned her best friend Ruth, breaking down in tears, to get advice and reassurance that things would be OK. Being a nurse, Ruth took Aunt Bess' number and rang her straight away to find out what the doctor had told them. Jenny was now settled and getting ready for bed. Her mother said to her calmly.

Being aware that Jenny was sensitive to her mother's feelings, Merla reassured her by saying, "Uncle Harry is unwell, but Aunt Bess said she is hopeful he's going to get better soon. Aunty Ruth is going to find out more for us and as soon as I know more I will let you know - OK?"

She nodded, and said, "Yes mum", but Merla thought deeper about how this news could affect a child and how she may be truly feeling. She wasn't sure if she was burdening a young child with bad news that may affect her psychologically in the future.

She then rang Mrs Green and gave her the bad news. Then it was Raymond's turn. Both were sorry to hear the news. They tried to console here but this was life and although they both wished they could make things better for her, it was impossible. Nobody, no matter how positive their experiences, go through life without some negative experiences or losses. It is said, *'It's through the negatives that one appreciates the positives'.*

Over the next two weeks, the situation was tense for Merla especially since Uncle Harry had his operation. The operation had gone well and he was making good progress. Every day she rang Aunt Bess to get the latest news and as the days went by Merla felt less anxious and more hopeful. Meeting Raymond for lunch and sharing her concerns with him also helped her. They sometimes met for lunch in a restaurant or grab a sandwich and took this to one of the parks dotted around their offices.

"Are you busy this weekend? I really want to take you and Jenny out. If you don't mind I would dearly love to meet her that is if you think she is ready to meet me".

"Funnily enough", Merla said, "I was thinking of letting you meet her as she has been wondering who I have been talking to every evening. Why don't you come round to dinner at my place on Saturday evening? That way she will be in her own environment and we can all feel more relaxed. If we all get on fine, we can maybe go out the following week, but I think before you take us out, we should see if you are wasting your money or not," she said jokingly.

They were definitely getting closer as their feelings for each other were growing and they were becoming more tactile. He squeezed her hands and they hugged each other when they parted.

"That sounds like a good idea", replied Raymond. "What time?"

"Oh leave that for now and I will let you know, but it's likely to be around 4.30pm as Jenny isn't used to being up late at nights". She returned to work with butterflies in her stomach.

Collecting Jenny, she casually told her that the person she has been talking to is coming to dinner on Saturday. What she was going to cook on Saturday occupied her mind. Knowing what drinks to buy was also a challenge as she hardly ever drank alcohol. The place needed cleaning so she started to spring clean the flat in the evenings, as the Saturday had to be free for cooking.

Saturday came and she prepared pumpkin soup for starters, ackee and salt fish, rice and peas and salad bowl. For the dessert, she made home-made fruit salad. Raymond arrived precisely at 4.30pm with flowers and a bottle of wine.

Greeting him with a kiss, she said. "Welcome darling to our abode. Have you been waiting outside for 4.30pm to arrive? You are exactly on time."

"No … just a stickler for good time keeping".

"What would you like to drink?"

"Jenny, our guest has arrived!"

"If you have red wine, I'll have that. If not, may I please have a beer? Do you have Red Stripe?"

"No, but I have red wine. You know not in a million years would I have bought Red Stripe beer. Jenny, this is Raymond, a very good friend of mine".

Awkwardly she shook his hand and went to help her mother in the kitchen. She really was a hindrance but was much too shy to stay in the living room with a stranger.

They sat down to eat and Merla asked if the wine was OK. "What about my pumpkin soup? I won't ask you about the ackee and salt fish as you can't really mess that up".

On finishing dinner, Raymond tried to strike up a conversation with Jenny by asking her banal questions such as "What are the names of your friends at school? What are your favourite book and your favourite television programme?" It was obvious this was a new experience for him as his questions to a child were mundane.

Jenny then asked him "Where do you live?"

"I don't live that far from here, in a flat similar to yours". They talked for a while and eventually Jenny retreated to her room to continue the single-child syndrome of playing with her toys and talking to her dolls.

The couple sat closely on the same settee with the television on but with it turned down low so they could talk quietly.

"Thank you for inviting me to meet Jenny, and you can cook! I thought you said you could just manage spag-bol! I really enjoyed your cooking".

"It's a little like 'Come Dine with Me' - you make the effort don't you when you know someone is coming for dinner? Cooking just for myself and a child means I don't usually make much effort".

"Since we met, I find myself thinking about you every day. I know I should not be saying this as your head might swell. We have become friends and I feel you are also attracted to me just as much as I am attracted to you. I swear my feelings for you are genuine; I really want to take our relationship further Merla", he said tenderly.

She wasn't really shocked by his comment as Merla felt the same way but wasn't sure if she should play hard to get or reciprocate his physical affection which would eventually mean they may end up making love at some point soon. Her emotional pendulum swung both ways: she wanted to go further with him, but with a cloud of doubt as to whether it was too soon; whether he was the right person, and with Jenny in the next room, she decided it was not right at that moment and decided not to move any closer to him.

Merla gently let him down by saying, "I also feel strongly for you and you have been just great over the past few weeks, but my frame of mind is not right for that at the moment and plus Jenny is here. I don't feel comfortable going any further at the moment. Sorry".

"That's alright - let me know when you are ready," he said with a smile. They talked and when it was time for Jenny to go to bed, he said goodnight.

"Thanks for coming and meeting Jenny," She said as she kissed him goodnight.

Work was going from strength to strength and everyday she was learning more and more about how she needed to work independently. As time went by, she was taking charge of more files with less supervision and Cyril was having even more confidence in her ability. Efficiency meant Merla had to forego something and that was her friendships, although Raymond was still a part of her life. True friends understood her situation, and were not offended if their calls were brief or she took a while to call them back. She always responded eventually.

Weeks went by and as she had more commitment, with the weekend chores and looking after Jenny, she could only invite Raymond for dinner on a Saturday evening. This time she cooked something less time-consuming, which was an indication that she was getting used to him and becoming more relaxed in his presence. Both consumed a bottle and a half of red wine, which over the evening may seem a lot, but wasn't really as neither was drunk. As she prepared Jenny for bed, Merla thought carefully to herself. "If we end up in the bedroom, I'll be fine with that. I am ready to take this further. I won't be making the first move however".

As she returned to the lounge, she joined him on the sofa. They watched television, which was pointless, as they weren't really concentrating on any programme. They began to kiss passionately and they were now staring into each other's eyes without a word uttered. Both said nothing but it was obvious they were ready to make love. By the time they reached the bedroom door, there was no going back. Raymond came prepared just in case the *inevitable* happened. The lovemaking was passionate and relatively short. As they lay on the bed, both turned to each other, still in a stupor, kissing, caressing and smiling and now realising they had sealed their relationship with love. As they lay there, an aerial view on her face conveyed a woman whose eyes, glazed with ardour, was in a good place.

She could not help herself when she asked him. "So do you always travel with a '*love glove*?"

"No but if you felt the same way as I did, I knew I was ready and I always remember what the Boys Scout taught me: 'Be prepared'. They both laughed. When it was time to leave Raymond kissed her and acknowledged what a wonderful evening he had.

CHAPTER 4

Merla and Raymond's relationship continued to grow stronger and both were now going to church although not as regular as Raymond would like. Merla still had motherly chores to carry out on Sundays. She also wanted to make a point that she would decide for herself when and if she went to church.

Uncle Harry had recovered enough for Merla not to worry as much. The promise to visit Aunt Bess and Uncle Harry was still on the cards however. At the start of the summer, Jenny kept reminding her mother about this. The holiday was booked for two weeks, but Jenny wasn't told as she would get even more excited.

As the holiday approached, Merla realised she needed to buy Jenny some new clothes as she had grown so big since last year. She was now 8 years old. They went shopping for new summer dresses and t-shirts. As a typical busy mother, she was still able to choose her daughter's clothes, so they went into a large chain store that sold the lot and bought everything there.

"These things I am buying you are not to be worn next week, so please don't ask. Understand?"

"Are these for my holiday?" she asked her mum.

"Maybe", her mother retorted with a smile.

Their holiday was fast approaching so it was time to clear her desk and update her boss on outstanding files. This holiday was really needed but

Merla could not help wishing it hadn't come around so quickly. Leaving work late on the last day, she hoped she would have got a seat on the train but no such luck. It was standing room only and if she didn't push to get on, she would still be waiting on the platform at least for another hour for a less crowded train. She was exhausted but consoled herself with the reality that she would be having a good rest very soon.

Suitcases were already packed. On the departure day, she woke Jenny early and said: "Why is mummy waking you this time of the morning? It's holiday time!" A beam on her face was all that Merla needed.

As they travelled to the airport, they sang to shorten and make the journey less arduous. They arrived on time. Merla noticed how late comers dashed/ scurried through the corridors, shouting 'sorry' or 'excuse me' as they pushed past other travellers to catch their flights. Families with pushchairs and hand luggage waited patiently to check in. The security check-in moved quickly as they opened more barriers. A big bugbear for Merla was the manner in which the airport designed the walkway towards the lounge by duping passengers to walk deliberately through the duty free areas, to entice them to spend their money before reaching the departure lounge. She sent Raymond a romantic text and instead of texting back, he phoned her with an adoring response.

The well-travelled business-person with hardly any luggage at all, walked confidently towards quiet spots where they charged their mobiles or used their laptops to fine-tune their presentations or reports.

When it was time to board, the first class passengers nonchalantly walked straight up to the front of the queue and boarded the plane. This was when Merla wished she was rich and could afford first class flights.

The plane took off on time at 9.00am. Jenny was now at the age where she understood aeroplanes and holidays, as it was something they talked about in the playground. Because of the time difference, they arrived in the middle of the day to face the sweltering heat. Aunt Bess sent a taxi for them. There was an alternative route up to the house, which means they wouldn't have to walk for ages in the heat. Aunt Bess was on the veranda waiting to greet them. It was now a few years since she had seen Jenny, and although she had seen photographs, she couldn't believe how she had grown. Merla hugged and kissed Aunt Bess and immediately went in to find Uncle Harry. Although now fit and well, he was lounging in the settee.

"The afternoon sun takes it out of me", he said as he got up to give her a big hug. "I cannot believe this is Jenny. Goodness what a way she has grown!"

"Say hello Jenny. Do you remember who this is?"

"Yes" Jenny said with a smile.

"How are you keeping Uncle?" asked Merla.

As usual, with his usual phlegmatic demeanour and uttering very few words, Uncle Harry responded. "I'm feeling well my dear. It's good to see you both. How long you are here?"

"We're really here to visit you folks. I should have come before now but Aunt Bess suggested to come after you came out of hospital. We're here for two weeks but I am going to visit a friend for two days and she is staying at a hotel on the coast when she comes over on holiday. Will let you know when but I'm here to see you folks, rest, help you folks and for Jenny to re-connect with the family".

"Are you folks hungry?" asked Aunt Bess.

"I'm just thirsty," said Merla.

"What about you Jenny?"

"No thank you, but could I please have a drink".

"Here you are my love," said Aunt Bess with an endearing smile.

They chatted and Merla gave the family a run-down of what has been happening in their lives. "Jenny has really settled into her school, made friends and I am coping as, although I am now training to be a solicitor, I try and organise myself at weekends, the best I can. Thank God, everything is falling into place. He has been very good to us."

Merla hadn't laden herself down with unnecessary gifts as she did the last time as she was conscious she had to look after Jenny while travelling. After all, with Uncle Harry not working or not working as regularly as he would normally like, they needed extra help financially so Merla brought them money. Immediately she gave them the cash and explained that regardless of what they thought, they would have money for the next few months. She promised them also that she would go food shopping tomorrow as she did on her last visit. The food grown on the island was delicious and she hankered after some of the perishable food not found in the UK, but she also wanted to have wine and *proper* bottled water.

"Is Metro supermarket still there?"

"Of course - and now they have an even bigger selection. They have expanded, selling more American food produce."

"Well are you doing anything tomorrow? You can come with me, if you are not busy. Uncle Harry won't want to come. He's never liked shopping at the best of times. It was a cultural thing as well: usually men that age don't shop with their wives. What time do Eddie and Gloria come home? I have presents for them, as I think they would prefer gifts. Now they are big people hopefully they will like them. I think these may be the last presents I'll be able to buy for them as people their age don't like what adults buy."

Being much older Jenny was now aware of her environment. She got bored with the adult conversation so said to her mother. "Can I please watch television?"

Her mum said, "Sorry love, the television is different to what you normally watch at home. There are few cartoon programmes, no Cartoon Network, "Crackerjack", "Sesame Street" here. "Anyway you are not here to watch television," her mum said with a smile. "We are going to eat some lovely fresh food and go to the beach as well as spend time with the family".

Aunt Bess said, "My dear just as well you aren't relying on the television; pure rubbish and American repeats. The American programmes teach our children bad behaviour with all the shootings and stabbings, far too materialistic and most of them do not speak proper English. In fact you can't understand a word they are saying". The poor then feel inadequate without the designer labels and then start to steal things. So fed up with it; I would love to see a sensible programme now and again. I know it has a lot to do with not having the money for sensible programmes, but the programme planners don't seem to care. I don't know where they learn their trade! Even the news readers - I think they are all friends who give each other jobs!" She said with a smile.

"The trouble is, people just accept things over here; they don't complain and that's why - not just the TV programmers, but the government, get away with nonsense," said Merla.

Defending them Aunt Bess said, "People just don't know how to complain, who to go to. Remember the majority of people are simple, they just about know how to read and write so we can't be too hard on them! It's a luxury to have the time to complain. People are too busy thinking where the next meal will come from or how they will pay their bills. The bright ones have left the country to go to overseas universities, settled in other countries where there are more opportunities and better-paid jobs. They call it the brain drain."

"I hear what you are saying but don't you get fed up with the way people operate and the way they just acquiesce to their circumstances?" asked Merla.

"Of course we do, but life is much too short to let these people make my blood pressure rise and with the sun, I try and not let people stress me out. I cannot afford to be sick, so take things in my stride. I believe many people just accept things, not because they don't know better, but just cannot be bothered. They don't think they can make any difference". Inefficiency and disorganisation is a big part of the society. Blame the so-called politicians who are supposed to be superior thinkers as they profess to be better-educated. They couldn't run a bath!"

Chatting away Eddie 18 and Gloria 17, now taking their A levels and hoping to go to university, were nearly home and this meant it was almost dinnertime. Aunt Bess had already cooked dinner. Merla's favourite: ackee and salt fish.

Merla smiled "You remembered".

"Remembered what?"

"My favourite food"!

"If I had forgotten that, it would mean I am going senile. I remember you would have eaten this every day if you had your way".

Merla thanked and hugged her Aunt. "Of course I could eat this every day, but my yearning for this is even more heightened as it's expensive in the UK, you can't buy it fresh; only tinned ones are available and even then I don't always see them in the shop".

As they expected their guests, Eddie and Gloria arrived home on time. Excitedly they greeted their relatives with hugs and kisses. They opened their presents with even more enthusiasm. Each got the latest trainers and sports tops. Merla made life easy on herself by buying the same thing so there would be no fuss. These were items which would make them the envy of their friends. Merla was a savvy shopper so she would have bought them in the sale or a discount shop. They were happy with their gifts so that was a relief all round.

After dinner and more chatting, Merla prepared Jenny for bed with the usual book-reading and mother-daughter exchanges and cuddles. Both liked this moment and it settled Jenny, who was extremely tired with the flight and the time difference.

Early morning was shopping day. Merla and company hailed a cab, which screeched as it made its way round the bend. She was ready to buy all the things that Aunt Bess thought was either too exorbitant or unnecessary for the home. Merla wasn't going to the market this time as she now hated the hassle and bartering exchanges. She also didn't want to waste all day outside as the sun would start to beat down on their heads come midday. Even with sun hats and flimsy clothing, it was still unpleasant for someone not used to the heat. Once upon a time, she could not have understood women with umbrellas in the sun, but now it made sense.

She spent the next few days helping to clean the house and cooking. Again, she wondered what the cleaner did, as all the rooms were superficially clean. She told Aunt Bess and Uncle Harry about Raymond, the important man in her life, work and her plans. They didn't quite comprehend the process of her job, but got excited anyway especially when Merla told them about Raymond.

"So tell me what Raymond is like? He sounds like a lovely young man."

"He is, but it's relatively early days so I don't know how this will go as yet," she replied cautiously and casually. Merla was beginning to have second thoughts about telling them about Raymond, as she knew what they would be like. Thereafter she was careful not to make their relationship sound too heavy or serious. Aunt Bess did however get excited when she heard Raymond was a Christian. To her that meant he was a *good man*. Aunt Bess just wanted Merla to be happy and have a good life. She was also worried that Merla was on her own with Jenny in a foreign land and wanted her to settle down and to have someone to take care of them. That generation had the same old-fashioned mentality that women were the home-makers and their husbands were supposed to take care of them. If a woman didn't find a man that meant she was unhappy and her life was missing something significant.

The following week her friend, Natalie, phoned to let her know she was staying at the Picasso Hotel in town. Merla phoned the hotel to book a couple of days for herself and Jenny. This meant she didn't have to worry about returning if they wanted to go out in the evenings for a meal or just to catch up on life. It would have been easy to leave Jenny with Aunt Bess but she wrenched with her conscience and guilt won the argument that she should take Jenny. She convinced herself she wanted Jenny to see another side of the island. The hotel faced the beach but there was the usual pool outside of the room. Jenny preferred the pool as she had just learnt to swim and she could practise there. That also pleased Merla who could sit with a book, or chat to her friend.

Natalie was a single 28-year old woman whose goal was to travel to as many countries as possible before she settled down. She had enjoyed her life since leaving university and started working. She managed a department within a large bank. Natalie didn't see anything wrong in holidaying on her own, but was astute enough to be careful on her choice of countries and hotels. Both women met a year ago when they attended a professional training day course. They struck up a friendship, which has lasted and now and again, they met up for lunch.

On arriving at the hotel Merla, unpacked her bags and she and Jenny went to the reception to find out the room Natalie was staying.

"Hi beauty, how are you keeping? Jenny...meet my friend Natalie".

"I've heard so much about you Jenny. Are you enjoying your holiday?" asked Natalie.

"Yes thanks", she replied.

"She looks so much like you Merla. So how's it going girl?" she turned to Merla.

"Things are going fine. We've been here nearly a week and been helping to clean up and shop for my Aunt and Uncle, so haven't been anywhere but hopefully we will get some rest now and have some fun. How about you - what you been up to since we last met?"

"It's just been work, work and more work. That's why I had to get away as I was beginning to walk around like a zombie! Sometimes I felt like I've sold my soul to the company. New people coming in, changes constantly taking place and these are all beyond my control. I just have to get on with it I suppose and do what I can. How is it on the man front?" asked Natalie getting straight to the point.

"Well I have met this guy called Raymond - he's 29. He is a darling but I'm not going to get too excited as its early days yet. He is charming, a traditionalist, and a likeable kind of person. He is an Accounts Manager in the City but I cannot understand why he hasn't been snapped up long ago. I think I have an idea why he is still single. Raymond knows what he wants and I don't believe any girl could have forced him into a situation if he didn't want to be there. I am quite laid back about it, as I have to concentrate on Jenny and work. Unfortunately, it's in that order for now. He is very understanding and I told him frankly, immediately we met. What about you?"

"My dear, everyone I meet starts off great then after a while a great big disappointment descends on the relationship. I am giving men a rest for a while. Don't need any more stress in my life. The problem for me is as I get older, my expectations rise, and I am becoming more set in my ways. For now, I'm single and loving it! "What do you fancy doing today?"

"We are easy, - don't mind as long as we eat later! What about you?", asked Merla.

"I think it's unanimous - food later. We could just lay by the pool today. It's lovely, cool, and not as busy in the afternoons as most of the holidaymakers are down at the beach. Tomorrow we could take a trip somewhere", suggested Natalie.

"I promised I would take Jenny to the Green Grotto Caves in Runaway Bay. It's a place I have heard about and passed when going to Dunn's River, but never visited. A friend of mine went there and told me it's worth a visit especially for Jenny. It's going to be cool down there plus it's a natural attraction".

"I'm up for that. We can book transport at the reception desk".

The women put on their swimsuits and all went for a swim in the pool. Having done a few laps they decided to paddle near the edge to have a chat while Jenny continued to swim. Both exited the pool and sat to the side while Jenny stayed in the water.

"Do you go to parties?" Natalie asked Merla.

"No, I was never a party animal. I'm what you'd call an old fogey. I like listening to music but really, I am not a great dancer. In fact, I never really got the practice. You see growing up in what people consider a religious environment, dancing, and music were considered much too secular. The nearest I got to music was the hymn book!"

"Well I used to enjoy parties and clubs but I'm bored with all that now. I just don't know where to meet nice men". The ones in the club aren't husband material and as I get older, I am more discerning. I am destined to be single. Sometimes even in a social setting, I feel lonely and bored. My friends are great but as they get married, they drop off as they have other interests. Not being big headed but people often look at me and think, 'she must have a boyfriend', but little do they know," said Natalie ruefully.

"Maybe you should take the bull by the horns and find one on the internet. I know some people who have done that and they have found compatible partners and are now happy", said Merla.

"I thought about that but then I chicken out at the thought of meeting some weirdo. They embellish their story and show a photograph taken ten years ago! It makes you wonder why they haven't been snapped up if they are so great. To me going on the internet to find a man smacks of desperation. I still believe in the conventional way of meeting a partner".

Merla replied, "Not necessarily. Remember if a man is busy with a demanding job, he won't have the time to meet a woman. It's just the stress of life nowadays. If you can't meet a suitable partner in your workplace, it's difficult outside of work. You just think about yourself and how stressful and demanding your job is, when are you going to find time to meet a man?"

"How did you meet Raymond?"

"I met him through a mutual friend at a dinner party. I wasn't looking for a man but we just connected. If this relationship doesn't work out, when I am ready to settle down, I'll consider internet dating".

"Do you think he could be the one?" asked Natalie.

"Yes, but I'm not getting too excited as we haven't reached that stage yet. I would say I more than like him, as he is very gentle, loving, and considerate. We'll see".

They returned to their rooms and arranged to meet for dinner later at a restaurant just about 25 yards down the road from the hotel. The restaurant was patronised by the locals and therefore much cheaper and tastier. The blaring reggae music and the jerk chicken roasting on the skewer led them to the restaurant. They ordered the jerk chicken, rice and peas, and salad, washed down with rum punch and fruit juice for Jenny.

"This is the life!" they joked as their conversation competed with the blaring music for attention.

"Quietness would seem inappropriate as the music added to the ambience. Don't you think?" asked Natalie.

Not wanting to seem a spoilsport, Merla said, "Totally agree - tranquillity should be left at the hotel", retorted Merla.

They returned and arranged, via the hotel, for transport to the Green Grotto Caves the next day. It would be an early start and they were tired, so they went to bed relatively early.

After breakfast, the women and Jenny boarded the minibus, sitting at the back so they could chat without too much interruption. As Merla didn't often meet up with friends, when she got into her stride, there was no holding back. Thank goodness Jenny had brought her portable games. Although the journey was a good distance, it did not seem too arduous with their chatter.

The entrance to the Green Grotto Caves was nondescript and they could easily have missed it if they were on their own. If it wasn't that the place came highly recommended, the entrance wasn't a convincing advertisement. This would never have happened in America or Europe, where signs for direction to the Caves would be in place miles before reaching them and on getting there, you would know you had arrived. As they descended the stairs, they realised how special the place really was, with even weddings and filming taking place there. Tourists were never told that the Green Grotto Caves was a *must* place to visit.

It was among the most prominent natural attractions on the island, featuring a large labyrinth of limestone caves. Filled with numerous rock formations, stalactites, and stalagmites and getting its name from the green algae that covered the walls, the Green Grotto, according to history, was a haven for runaway slaves, gunrunners, and Spanish soldiers in the 18th century. The innermost cavern contained a crystal-clear underground lake. Jenny was fascinated and her mother tried to explain as much as possible but it was obvious that all the information was too much for her to comprehend.

The minibus then took them to a riding school as they had a lot of time left. This was another new experience for Merla and Jenny. Jenny on a pony and Merla on a horse rode through the countryside. What was concerning to Merla wasn't so much the fact that the horses appeared bigger than she thought, but the pathways were uneven and she feared the horses may become excited as they cantered down the gravel pathways. For part of the journey, they were taken to an inlet where the horses paddled through the water while the riders clung on for dear life. Eventually the riders became accustomed to the ride and just when they were enjoying this, it all ended. Natalie refused to go on the horse and was happy to read her book in the minibus. When it was time to leave, everyone was so tired they sat in silence as the minibus made its way back to the hotel.

The next day they relaxed and stayed local, enjoying lazing on the white sandy beach and continuing with their catching up. Both women agreed to meet some time in the near future during lunch or for a weekend dinner. In the evening Merla and Jenny returned to Aunt Bess's house.

Aunt Bess was so glad they had returned. If she had her way, they wouldn't have gone away for two nights. Being young at heart, she really appreciated conversations with Merla who was now much more worldly and could keep her abreast of current events. She loved the fact that Merla was ambitious and Jenny had settled down in a new country and a new environment. She acknowledged to Merla how pleased she was with what she had done, all on her own. It was the sort of affirmation Merla had always sought, and she basked in the realisation that she wasn't doing a bad job after all.

The time had flown so quickly, that before they realised it, the two weeks holiday was nearly over and it was time for them to return home. Uncle Harry was now better but Merla was mindful she needed to send them money more often as Eddie and Gloria were now adults and Uncle Harry couldn't work as hard as he used to, yet they needed more things. She was worried about the extra responsibility but had no choice as Eddie and Gloria were planning to go to university and would need financial help, even although they worked weekends and holidays, when they could get jobs.

They spent the last day packing and their suitcases were lighter than when they arrived. Merla was extremely sad; mortality was at the forefront of her mind as she wasn't sure when she would see them again. These thoughts had never crossed her mind before. She kept the morbid thoughts to herself and tried to put a positive spin on her farewell, telling them she would be back soon and next month she would be sending them some money.

They were soon at the airport and on the plane. The flight was smooth and the plane touched down the following morning. It seems as if they have been travelling for ages, but thank goodness, Jenny slept on the plane. Bittersweet feelings overwhelmed Merla: she was missing her close family but on the other hand, she was glad to be home and was looking forward to seeing Raymond again soon.

The couple spoke immediately on her landing. "Next time you go I am coming. I missed you so much - you will never know." What did I do before you entered my life? We spoke but it wasn't the same," said Raymond.

"I thought you would have enjoyed the time without me, watching football, going to the gym or doing whatever." She said while smiling. I can't wait to see you either. I'm off tomorrow as we are still jet-lagged and then I'm returning to work the following day for a couple of days. Do you fancy coming round on Saturday? I don't promise you any fancy dinner but we could get a take-away." Merla said.

Raymond retorted, "What do you think love? I can't wait - see you at around 4/5ish?"

The following day, Merla and Jenny had a lie-in, then unpacked and did their washing. Luckily it was a nice day and although not tropical weather, the clothes dried by late evening.

The usual preparation was made for herself and Jenny for her return to work early the next morning. It was an adjustment running down the escalator to catch the morning train. Those lucky enough to get a seat had their eyes glued in a book or the daily newspaper. After smiles and greetings, she bonded herself to her desk trying to catch up with phone calls, emails, and correspondence. Cyril was pleased to see her return, not only because he liked her, but also because she would help to lighten his workload. "I hate to think how much work I would have had on my desk if I'd gone away for a month!", she said to Cyril.

"What are you talking about, you're not allowed a whole month off in one go!" Cyril retorted jokingly.

On collecting Jenny, she spoke to Mrs Green who agreed to keep Jenny on Saturday from the afternoon onwards. She knew Raymond would want her to himself on Saturday. Merla had now started taking the pill so any worries of unwanted pregnancy were out of the way. She was now taking control of her life and her future. Why should she not enjoy sex with the man she cared for? She was surprised how much she missed Raymond.

The bell rang at 4.30pm. A big smile coupled with caresses and kisses greeted Raymond.

"I missed you so much," Raymond said between kisses. "You're lucky I didn't come and meet you as there's no way you were going to get away with a restrained peck on the cheek even with Jenny there!"

They didn't even wait for formalities such as having a drink beforehand. They had strewn their clothes all over the floor on their way into the bedroom. They kissed and cuddled making passionate love. Lying on the bed looking at the ceiling, their eyes still radiated in the splendour of the post-sexual fervour. They cuddled as they talked, reflecting on how much they missed each other.

Kissing him, Merla said, "We are both adults and know what we want". "I want you".

"I want to have you every day in my life," replied Raymond. "It doesn't make any difference how long we have been going out or how long we know each other. We know each other more than a lot of couples as since meeting you, we have talked and talked. I can't get you out of my head. I know you more than you think darling and I love what I see!" he added.

"You're a right sweet-talker. If I didn't know you better, I'd think you have just read a love story," she said smiling.

"I have - I'm experiencing *my* love story", he replied.

They got up, dressed, and phoned for pizza, finishing a bottle of wine. While they ate, Merla updated Raymond on her trip and her family. The couple watched a little television, played music, and returned to bed. Both fell asleep in each other's arms and didn't wake up until the next day.

After breakfast, he left and Merla collected Jenny. Mrs Green was happy to see Merla and she could see that her face displayed love and contentment.

Mrs Green, a mature and wise woman, just diplomatically asked, "How's Raymond?"

"He's fine thanks", was the response, killing any idea of a prolonged detailed reply.

Hand in hand going home, Merla said to Jenny, "What do you think about Raymond"?

Jenny said, "He's nice. Is he coming round today?"

"No - I saw him last night. What do you mean by nice?" she pressed for a more in-depth answer.

"He's our friend and he plays with me while you are cooking; he's fun".

"Great - glad you said that love".

They walked in silence the rest of the journey hand in hand.

Merla spent the entire week catching up on her workload. Although she was tired in the evenings, she spoke to Raymond nearly every evening; endeavouring also to speak to a couple of her friends to update them on her trip.

As the weekend approached, Raymond said he would like to see her.

"OK but Jenny will be here," she said.

"I would love to see Jenny - haven't seen her for a while".

Raymond bought a present for Jenny. He was aware that he usually brings wine and flowers but Jenny never got a personal present, so he bought her an electronic game. In a bag, he also brought a bottle of chilled wine, flowers, and three "Wedding" books for Merla.

After greeting Jenny and giving her the present, he still had the bag. He took out the flowers and wine, hugging, and kissing Merla.

Being a typical inquisitive woman she asked, "What have you got in that bag?"

"Never you mind, nosey Parker", he said smiling.

"I haven't got anything fancy for dinner; just some fish and cabbage. Want to join us?"

"Would love to; your food is always great."

"I'm going to finish off the dinner with some rice and vegetables so you can either keep my company or relax in the living room with Jenny".

"Think I'll go and play with Jenny, she's more fun", he said jokingly.

They ate dinner in peace, without much talking.

"Compliments to the chef - thanks darling. That was delicious. Now you go and sit down with your daughter and I'll clear up and wash the dishes".

"Are you sure?" asked Merla, feeling uncomfortable about the offer to wash up as it really wasn't her style to make a guest do the dishes after a meal.

"Of course I'm sure", he said.

They watched television and later with Jenny gone to bed, they continued to talk, played Luther Vandross' *'So Amazing'*, and other romantic songs then he said.

"You wanted to know what I had in the bag. Well I brought you some magazines".

"Why the delay and mystery?" "How bizarre", she thought.

He opened the bag and got out the three "*Wedding*" magazines.

Awkwardly she said, "What is this? You know I don't read magazines". The penny hadn't dropped as yet as Merla was a little slow and always thought he was too literal for any games. After a delay in his response she asked, "Am I thinking right? …Are you asking me to marry you?" she asked with a curious smile on her face.

"Exactly, will you marry me?" He went down on one knee with one of the magazine in his hands.

She laughed, "That's the cheapest engagement present I've ever seen!"

She looked at him, hesitated, kissed him, and said "Yes. You great big romancer - of course yes," she sealed the answer with another kiss.

"Where's the engagement ring?" asked Merla.

"Well I didn't want you to reject me and I wasted my money buying a diamond ring." He laughed.

"Very sensible but a little unromantic", said Merla. "Actually, can I come with you when you're buying it? After all I'm going to be wearing it for a long while so I should choose it."

"And you call me unromantic. Of course you can come. I have no experience of this kind of thing so great you'll pick the ring. It will also save time on resizing but most importantly, you will get the opportunity to choose what you want."

"When do you want us to go?" asked Merla enthusiastically.

"I can't do next Saturday as I am taking Jenny to a birthday party. We could go the following week, taking Jenny with us. After all she is a part of the celebration".

They kissed goodnight and promised to keep it their secret for now.

Merla went to bed with a smile on her face. She slept peacefully and was itching to tell Jenny the next day, but she didn't. Inside she was extremely happy and realised how difficult it was to keep this a secret. The couple spoke every day after she was finished doing her chores. They already made a pact only to text each other during lunchtime, as their other daily contacts were becoming distracting.

Over the next two weeks, Merla looked in all the jewellery shops she passed, hoping to get some ideas as to what she liked. She thought she wanted a solitaire but wasn't sure on the cut or whether to have white or yellow gold. She thought white gold was more contemporary, but if she found something in yellow gold, which was beautiful, she would go for that. She knew once she chose a ring that was it so it was important to pick the right one.

That Saturday she and Jenny met Raymond and they went shopping in Hatton Garden, London.

"Darling I hope you have come prepared," she whispered.

"Prepared for what?"

"For walking and I hope you haven't forgotten your wallet!" Merla grinned.

"I'm prepared - see I'm wearing my trainers. As for the money, I have my favourite friend", he smiled, pointing to his credit card.

They looked in nearly all the jewellers, dismissing outright the ones that didn't suit them, and making a mental note of the ones they liked. A couple of rings really stood out as right for her and they ended up visiting the shops twice to try for sizing. Merla chose a 1.0-carat solitaire white gold ring and left Raymond inside the shop to barter on the price. She found this type of thing embarrassing but he relished the challenge, so she left him to negotiate while she and Jenny waited outside. He left the shop with a professionally packed bag and they went for lunch.

While they waited for their meal, Raymond took the ring out of the box and asked her again.

"Will you marry me? I'd love you to be my wife", he whispered.

"Yes", she said with a kiss.

On went the engagement ring and Merla showed her daughter the ring and explained its significance to her. She kept looking at the ring on her finger and kept smiling in between looking at Raymond.

"Who would have thought you and I would have ended up together? I wasn't even looking for love but what a wonderful outcome? I am very happy. Can we come to church with you tomorrow? If I'm going to become Mrs. Wilson I want to become a full part of your life and your church family. I really do love you," she whispered in Raymond's ears.

"Mum you told me it was rude to whisper in a crowd!" said Jenny.

"Sorry love, mum is wrong to do that. I think however, it is allowable if it so personal you don't want anyone else to hear. If you, for example, wanted to go to the toilet, you would whisper this to me, you wouldn't shout it out aloud for everyone to hear, would you?".

"OK - as you know church starts at 11.00am and I'll meet you outside 10 minutes before that - OK?" said Raymond.

"See you tomorrow and thanks for a wonderful day - not to mention the present you gave me!" she said looking at her finger, as they kissed goodbye.

On her way home, she took a notebook out of her bag and drew up a list of the friends she would be inviting to a celebratory dinner; to introduce Raymond to her friends and a dinner party was well overdue in any case. The first person she phoned to tell was Mrs. Green, her surrogate mother. She was so excited and pleased for her. Then she rang Ruth and Monty. They were not surprised about the engagement as they felt the two of them just clicked, and they looked as if they had been together for years.

As Raymond was a long-standing member and popular in the church, she knew the church family would be interested in her especially after church ended, but never imagined eyes would be staring at them throughout the entire service. It was however a lovely service and at the end, Raymond introduced his fiancé and her daughter to the well-wishers who wanted to meet them.

"Many congratulations". "So pleased to hear the good news" and we hope to see you again soon", were the repeated responses.

Merla realised that as they were now engaged, and she had met his church friends, she had to make a bigger effort to attend church with Raymond. She really did not mind as being engaged meant they should be a complete couple. She just had to change her weekend schedule to include this added commitment. They now realised how in love they were and could not bear the thought of excluding the other from their interests or friends. Ruth and

Monty also attended that church so it would not be that daunting for Merla, as she knew someone else there.

On arriving for work, she went straight into Cyril's office to give him the good news and to show him the ring.

"I'm so happy for you. Who is the lucky young man? What a whopper of a stone!" he joked.

She gave him a quick rundown of Raymond, and Cyril said that he looked forward to meeting him at one of their company's staff events. As she worked, her colleagues came up to her to congratulate her. Now and again, her ring distracted her from work, and as she looked at it, she was smiling inside. She was happy.

In the evening, she was in two minds to tell Uncle Harry and Bess as she knew after the news had sunk in and their elation settled, they would be asking "So when is the wedding? Where are you going to get marry? She phoned and told them, with the immediate statement that they wouldn't be getting married for now.

Typically, for Merla, the dinner invitation was informal. She took a photograph of herself looking at one of the copies of the "*Wedding*" magazine. On the back of the photograph, she wrote "Merla would like to invite you to a dinner party to introduce you to a special person; further details to be given on the day!" without any mention of an engagement. "See you on Saturday in two weeks time at 7.00pm. Let me know by next Saturday if you can/t make it".

On the Saturday of the dinner party, she commissioned Mrs Green to help her prepare the food. Mrs Green would be at the party and she knew about the engagement but as she hadn't yet met Raymond, she was excited. As her table wasn't large enough for the 12 people invited, Merla organised it to be a buffet-style dinner, with trays, crockery plates, and glasses. Laid out elegantly on the table were West Indian hard dough bread, salad, coleslaw, fried plantains, jerked chicken, fried fish, dumplings, and rice and peas. Drinks: red and white wine, beer, and soft drinks. The doorbell rang at

7.00pm sharp. The first guest had arrived and there was a steady flow for the next 5/10 minutes. The arrangement was for Raymond to appear at 7.30pm after all the guests had already arrived. By then they all had drinks and were feeling relaxed. Discreet music played in the background. Merla turned down the music when Raymond entered the room. She held his arms and said,

"This is Raymond Wilson, a wonderful man I met a year ago and we became engaged a few weeks ago. I am going to pre-empt the obvious question. We don't know when we will be getting married as yet as things happened so quickly. We are extremely happy and Jenny and I look forward to Raymond being a part of our future. I'll introduce you all to him individually. He won't remember all your names but with time, he will get to know you all. Food and drinks are on the table. Help yourself to as much as you want. There is more in the kitchen. Enjoy the evening!"

The women of course were more interested in the ring. "I bet you picked it didn't you Merla?" they joked as they stared at the ring.

The evening went well and everybody left by 11.00pm. By then Jenny was in bed so Merla and Raymond cleared up and enjoyed the rest of the night by themselves.

On Monday, she wanted to find out how Mrs Green felt about Raymond.

"I really don't know him but he looks like a sincere young man. You both seem to suit each other and look happy together so my dear, all I can say is may the good Lord bless you both and I hope you two will have a great future together. Nobody knows what the future holds, so just be positive and hope for the best".

"That's all I wanted to hear from you; thanks for your kind wishes". Merla kissed her.

Now settled into a routine of working hard and coming home to look after Jenny, Merla was only able to see Raymond weekends, either at church or on a Saturday. They did however speak on the phone every night, telling each other how the day went and what was bothering them. The training contract was going well. Before long, she would have completed part of her legal training, because her company took into consideration her previous legal executive experience. Merla was now 25, and Jenny was now eight, so she started to give Jenny extra work preparing her slowly for the eleven plus exam.

The couple planned to marry the following year and decided it would be a small inexpensive wedding. They also wanted to buy a house together before they got married. To accrue more money for the house deposit, they decided to sell one of their flats and rent out the other. Both names would be on the mortgages so the two properties were equally divided.

As the cold weather approached, she heard Uncle Harry was sick again but not as seriously as before. This time Merla contacted her fiancé, he came round, prayed for healing that he would get better soon. Her faith was growing, so once they prayed, she felt more at peace. His sickness concerned her, but she didn't worry as she did the first time round. If the situation didn't get worse, they decided they would all go over and spend Christmas with the family. Merla wanted them to meet Raymond before the wedding.

When Merla was on her own, she considered how life throws all sorts of bittersweet experiences at the human race. One minute she was ecstatic about her relationships and the progress she was making; the next moment she was worried about mortality. This made her realise how precious and important her relationship was with her family and particularly, Jenny and Raymond. Time was short and she intended to make a conscious effort not to take her relationships for granted.

To lighten one of their evening conversations, Merla asked Raymond, "What do you do with yourself in the evenings once we've finished our daily chat?" She knew how much work she had to do being a single mother, but wondered if his evenings were filled with pleasure pursuits, such as watching TV with friends or going to the gym.

"You'd be surprised to know my evenings go quickly, bringing work home, catching up with friends and family nonsense. You don't know how lucky you are to have your family abroad. I sometimes wish I didn't have to get involved with family feuds. In each family structure, consciously or subconsciously, certain family members are elected to take on certain roles. I have been awarded the family arbiter. My brother's role is the time-waster".

"How do you cope with their feuds then?", she asked.

Resigned to the situation he said, "I wouldn't mind if they were genuine quarrels, so we could try to resolve issues, but most are a storm in a teacup, or the same disputes come up time and time again. I listen and then I tell them I will hear what the other one has to say. It depends on how I feel. I sometimes believe these squabbles would die down if they were ignored. They sometimes become friends again without any intervention so I don't always pander to their complaints and arguments."

The couple decided to sell Merla's flat and buy a house in both their names, in the same area, as Merla still wanted to be close to Mrs Green who took care of Jenny. They also agreed for her to settle in the house with Jenny and sort it out while Raymond continued to live in his flat until they got married. In a traditional religious mindset, living together before marriage was an absolute no-no for Raymond. Although they had already slept together as adults, his traditional religious beliefs overrode contemporary standards and morals. Raymond saw marriage as showing respect to Merla and setting a good example to Jenny, not to mention his community and his family.

At weekends they started to view properties but with the trip to see Uncle Harry hanging over their heads. Should they buy before going or leave it until they returned? Both agreed if they really loved a property before they go, they would try to purchase beforehand or at least get the ball rolling. However, if nothing appealed to them, they would leave it and take their time to purchase on their return. It would just mean the New Year would mean both arranging a wedding and also purchasing a house. Ideally, they wanted to have the place decorated and sorted before they got married. What were they looking for?

Like most young couples, they wanted as much space as possible for their money. "The minimum bedrooms would be 3: one for the couple, another for Jenny and a spare room for the study and/or extra bedroom for guests. They wanted a largish kitchen, with lots of cupboards, bathroom, a dining room, and lounge. The house also had to be close to the station. The time of year meant prices were more competitive but they were surprised at the way house prices had increased. Both searched for houses on the websites and made weekend viewing appointments.

The phone rang one evening and it was Bess.

As she could detect anxiety and worry in Merla's voice Aunt Bess quickly said:

"Don't worry it's not bad news. He is out of hospital. I don't know what they gave him but he looks so much better. They thought it was an infection and they gave him antibiotics to clear it up. He is much better now, thank God".

"Did you get the money I sent?" asked Merla. "We are hoping to come over at Christmas to see the family and I'm bringing Raymond for you all to meet him. So glad that Uncle is feeling better and by then he will be completely better. We cannot all stay with you as there is not enough room for all of us, but we'll be there. I wanted to give you a surprise but on the other hand I know you prefer not to get that type of surprise".

"Thanks for the money. That will help us especially going to and from the hospital and paying for the medication. Bless you Merla. I can't wait to see you all again and look forward to meeting Raymond. Have I got his name right?"

"Yes, let me know what you want me to bring you all for Christmas as I have to start sorting it out now. With Raymond, I might be able to bring more. I'm bringing a cake as you know I love Christmas cake".

Finishing off the conversation, Merla was so relieved Harry was fine, and on hanging up, she immediately phoned Raymond to update him. They talked and laughed that evening and on finishing, Raymond said a little prayer thanking God that Harry was going to be OK. Although he was a very self-confident person, Raymond still believed there was a Higher Being who was ultimately in charge of everything and everyone.

The next weekend the couple looked at houses, and in the evening they took Mrs Green for dinner as it was her birthday. She was more than overdue for a 'thank you' dinner.

Slightly overdressed, Mrs Green looked elegant in her silk blouse and pearls, which meant Merla and Raymond felt underdressed, but 'that was a generational thing' they thought. Young people don't dress up for dinner nowadays as they are always dining out; it's become a regular event for them. They went to their local Indian restaurant, frequented by Merla and Raymond. Mrs Green hardly ever went to a restaurant, as she preferred her own home cooking. Having said that, she looked forward to going out with the couple, as this put her in touch with the wider world and thought it was such a lovely gesture. As they went early on a Saturday, the ambience was peaceful, but Raymond reassured Mrs G that it was not always like that and it would be busier later in the evening. Not that she minded. They started with glasses of wine with Jenny having orange juice, they then worked through the poppadoms, with mango chutney and tomato and chilli sauce, although the cucumber and mint wasn't as popular, nor the coconut relish. They had a wonderful afternoon and at the end, Merla produced out of her bag, a birthday card, a beauty voucher, and Mrs Green's favourite perfume, which a few weeks ago she remarked she needed to replace as it was running low after a couple years' usage. Mrs Green had a big grin on her face as she opened the presents.

"I wasn't giving you a hint you know! I shall cherish today and your kind gesture," she said laughing.

"Of course I know that, but just goes to show I do listen to every word you say! Thank you for being such a caring and helpful human being. We are so grateful to you for your help," retorted Merla.

The next few weekends were filled with viewing properties and *getting to know people* time for the couple. Raymond invited Merla and Jenny to one of his relative's Sunday dinner parties. Purposely in one swoop, she met his entire family. His sister, the midwife, was pleasant and quite chatty; his younger brother didn't have much to say, but that may be because the brothers' relationship was frosty. Merla found Raymond's mother warm and welcoming. To create a relaxed atmosphere, his father cracked jokes and then proceeded to laugh at his own jokes, to the annoyance of his wife. Merla also met a couple of aunties and cousins. One was working as a social worker and a couple of his cousins were young students. They all welcomed her and Jenny and made them felt relaxed.

"I won't remember all their names. Hope you don't mind. It's not that I don't care, I just forget names but remember faces. Did you brief them before I met them? "Just strange they didn't ask me many questions, especially your parents."

"I did tell my parents about you and Jenny and how you were both very important people in my life and we were now engaged. The message would have been passed on to the others I'm sure. It doesn't matter what they think. They know me well so won't ask too many questions as I will be blunt in my answer. I can manage the situation."

"I know it doesn't matter to you or me, but I hope they'll like me. We want to get off to a good start, don't we?" Merla said.

A couple of Saturdays later Merla and Raymond found the ideal house that ticked several of their boxes. With original features and high ceilings, the rooms were much larger than the others they had seen. The bathroom needed refurbishing but the newly fitted kitchen had room for a dining table. On top of that, there was an en suite bathroom attached to the main bedroom, which was like the icing on the cake. It was within walking distance of Mrs. Green's house, which meant once she got off the train, she could walk home with Jenny. It was also within their price range.

"What do you think love?" asked Merla.

"I think this one is fine for us as it fits most of our requirements; it will be suitable for now", said Raymond. Remember it is our first home together, so it's fine. With our budget, I don't think we are going to get anything better than this".

"OK we shall be going for this one then? You are right, for the money we have, we are getting a lot of house", said Merla.

They informed the estate agent of the proposed purchase and Merla got someone in her office to commence the conveyance work. They were now getting ready for the Christmas trip. It was a little early, but Merla liked to be prepared. In addition to taking a cake, she hoped to take chocolates and mince pies, all things Aunt Bess loved.

One evening, she came home tired and got the call she had always dreaded from Aunt Bess. It wasn't good news. Uncle Harry had suddenly died that day. Merla was overwhelmed with sorrow and hugged Jenny as she told her the bad news. Jenny mirrored her mother's sadness and began crying also. Getting on the phone, she told Raymond, Mrs Green and her best friends the sad news. This news brought forward their plans and immediately she realised she had to travel as soon as possible to help Bess with the funeral arrangements and to generally support her. Uncle Harry will now never meet Raymond and vice versa. He had worked tirelessly to support his family.

Raymond went round to her flat to support her in her loss. A cloud of sadness descended on her psyche, making her believe that with every wonderful things that has happened to her, she had to pay for with grief. In between tears, anxiety and concerns for the family she asked the following questions.

"Why us now? What happened? Why this sudden demise, God? Why oh why did you take him away from us? He didn't deserve to go now. He was such a good man. We shouldn't have lost him so soon. I really wanted him to be proud of me and I'm not going to get the chance now. I wanted him to meet you Raymond".

These questions perplexed Raymond as he tried to answer sagaciously, but he couldn't give her sensible, rational answers so he relented, hugged her, listened as she pondered and cried. "I'm sure he was proud of you darling".

The next day she arranged with her boss to take compassionate leave. She immediately booked her ticket for both she and Jenny. Raymond would be travelling later to support her, nearer the funeral date. He didn't want to just meet the family and immediately take charge of funeral arrangements. It was a new situation for him and he had to be compassionate and supportive to the family but he was just meeting them, unsure of individual characters in the family. "At funerals when everyone's emotions was at the fore and extremely sensitive, one had to proceed with caution. Nobody appreciates a stranger intruding into their lives at the time of a loss", he thought rather wisely.

Typically, she insisted on seeing her boss before she flew out, to brief and update him on her work, as she would be flying out within days. Going into work that day distracted her emotions temporarily. Just as well she had started to prepare for the trip early. The celebratory gifts now seemed inappropriate, but she was taking them anyway as they were already purchased and Aunt Bess and the others may draw comfort from these goodies. Merla bought another hat for Aunt Bess - this time black -and presents for Eddie and Gloria.

On arriving she was met by the same taxi driver Aunt Bess had arranged on her last visit. It was comforting to have someone meeting them who knew her Aunt. She couldn't deal with any other pressure now.

"You remembered me!" she said to him. "What's your name?"

"Cedric ma'am", he said subserviently.

"……..pleased to meet you again. My name is Merla and this is my daughter Jenny".

"I know why you're here. He was such a good man, very humble and friendly".

They hardly talked as he drove them to the house. She wasn't in the mood to converse as her thoughts were far away.

Aunt Bess met them on the veranda. With tears in her eyes, she said, "So glad you could make it - thanks for coming over. You will never know how grateful I am that you are here. How are you Jenny?" she hugged them both. "I wouldn't know where to start to arrange a funeral. We went to few but never in my wildest dream did I think I would have to go through this already".

"I had to be here. I want to be here. Raymond is coming in a few days' time, but I came as soon as possible to help with the arrangements."

"Let me ring Raymond and tell him we've arrived safely and then we can talk".

"What happened?" Merla asked.

"The morning he got up, he said he wasn't feeling well. He couldn't say what the problem was. You know what he is like. As the day went on, he kept asking for more painkillers. I wasn't happy with that so I told him we were going to the hospital. By the time the taxi came, he got worse and on reaching the hospital, he was gone; just like that! The doctor said he died from septicaemia."

"Poor man, thank God he didn't suffer for long." Merla said reassuringly.

"Well you say that but who knows how long he was suffering? We women if we feel pain, we express how we are feeling, but men they suffer in silence. It's a macho attitude they have; its frowned upon to express their emotions. They feel they shouldn't show any sign of weakness so they ignore whatever their body is telling them. Especially that generation.

Jenny kept a low profile, as she was aware of the intensity of the situation and went off to read her book. Her mother had also brought with her the eleven plus practice papers. Even in this state of affairs, Merla had her eyes on the ball.

They spent the rest of the day talking and considering how they would be financing the funeral. That was important as this loss came suddenly, and it was clear the responsibility would fall on Merla. Like most people of their age, living in the country, with limited means, the insurance policy they had for the funeral was highly unlikely to be sufficient and this wouldn't be paid out in time in any case. When Merla thought about death and funeral costs, she thought to herself, "Even in death the poor suffer. How on earth do they manage?"

"Well the service is going to be at the church we attend. He'll be buried on our farm as that is what he wanted. The first time he was sick that was what he requested. Our Minister will conduct the service and I know we have to get permission for him to be buried on the land. We also have a chef at church that can cater for the gathering after the funeral. You know we will have to cater for the whole church and I think members total approximately 150. That's how they do it over here" said Aunty.

"I know that's how they do it over here but I am a little cynical as although some will be there out of respect, a lot will be there for the free food. Anyway, we should cater for about 160, to avoid running out of food. We should be all right if we get the caterers to serve the food so the people won't help themselves to four pieces of chicken breasts instead of one or two!" said Merla with a smile.

"We need to get the stationery printed. Once we decide I'll ask Raymond to arrange and get him to bring it all with him, as he will know where to go to get the whole programme printed. That's the next thing we have to sort out. Let's sort out who will be saying what and who else would like to say something. We will need to ring them. Are there any others coming from abroad?"

"No" said Aunty.

"That will make it so much easier then. We won't need to delay the day of the service. Let me know what readings you and/or Uncle would like, and who should read them. By tomorrow I would like to have a draft programme ready so we can check and send to Raymond as he needs to get this printed." said Merla.

Unpacking her suitcase, she took out the presents she had brought for the family. This was a poignant time as they were sad but the presents did compensate for the situation they were now experiencing.

Many thanks for the hat. I think this will be ideal for the funeral, but I won't be wearing it as every time I wear it, I will remember the funeral", said Bess.

"Actually, I bought it for you to wear to church. Just glad you like it. Let's hope Gloria will like the dress and Eddie will like the shirt. What time do they get home?" Eddie was now in his first year at university studying Computer Science and Gloria in her final year taking her 'A' levels. "I am going to rest now as I got up so early this morning. Please wake me when they get home. Jenny, are you coming to lie down with mummy?"

"OK, but can I take my game with me in case I can't sleep?" said Jenny.

"In other words, you are going to keep me awake. You don't have to rest if you don't want to, but I know I want to lie down. Stay with Aunty if you wish".

"OK you go sleep," said Jenny as she exited the room.

Merla slept almost immediately and only woke up when Eddie and Gloria came home. The conversations taking place in the next room between Aunt Bess and the young people talking to Jenny interrupted her sleep.

Bleary-eyed she emerged, "Well I am going to state the obviously annoying thing adults like to say: you two have grown so big since the last time I saw you", Merla said greeting them with hugs and kisses. "I brought these for you - let me know if you like them or not", knowing full well they would not say they hated their presents. That wasn't the way they were brought up to behave.

Aunt Bess knew Merla was still tired so she told her to go back to bed as she would look after Jenny and put her to bed when she was tired.

Hesitating only for a minute, she took the opportunity and went straight back to bed and slept like a baby, as she was so tired. In the morning, she had a quick breakfast and went straight into finalising the programme.

"What songs would you like, or what songs do you think Uncle would have liked?"

"Well I think it's a mixture of what he liked and what I like and these are some of the ones we sung in church and at other funerals. I know some of them are going to start me crying. They are so emotional, but they are full of feelings and remind me of the love of our Heavenly Father", said Bess.

Amazing Grace

Great is Thy Faithfulness

How Great thou Art

Make me a Channel of your Peace

The Old Rugged Cross

When the Roll is Called up Yonder

There is a Green Hill Far Away

The Lord is My Shepherd

As Bess spoke, her voice was full of emotion as she was welling up inside. Merla wondered how she was going to manage the situation, but knew she had to do the programme. She tried to ignore the changing voice but as the emotions got stronger Merla said, while hugging her:

"We are going to find this difficult, so whenever you want a break or if you want to cry, cry. I will cry with you. Can you please let me have Pastor Morris' number so I can arrange to meet up with him? Ideally, I would like to meet him later today, that's why I need to do a mock-up to show him. Then I will send it off to Raymond for printing. I also have to compose the obituary. Let's see Pastor Morris first and in the meantime if you could think about what I should say about Uncle Harry write it down and I will put in some order."

"Well I will dig out some old papers, with the information of where he worked, and try to remember things like where we met, when we decided to get married and the kind of person he was. I know he was a loving, hard-working man and he did everything he could for his family. He was a proper family man; not proud and very quiet and understated. I'm going to miss him", said Bess.

Pastor Morris decided to come to the house to meet Merla that afternoon and he outlined how the funeral should be conducted. He also gave her contacts details for the mortician, catering and the gravedigger and Merla contacted them immediately after he left. Her reason for that was to get an estimate of the costs for all of these functions. She had slept for such a long time the previous night, so she did not go to bed until late that night, writing the obituary, choosing a photograph of Uncle Harry to be included in the programme. Then she sent the information to Raymond, requesting 150 programmes and 2 copies of the obituary. The next day they went to the mortician who could also arrange the flowers. She asked for the flowers to be unassuming, nothing garish, just cream lilies, and carnations with a few red roses.

In between the funeral planning, supporting Aunt Bess, and looking after Jenny, Merla was missing Raymond badly as physically he wasn't there to support her although they spoke daily.

Raymond arrived a few days later, and although he would be staying at the Picasso Hotel, he immediately took a taxi to Aunt Bess' house where, although Merla was overjoyed to see him, she hid her emotions and underplayed how much she had missed him. It was frowned upon, deemed as disrespectful to adults and parents to display too much emotion to your boyfriend when in the presence of adults, especially parents. Culturally this was uncomfortable for parents to see their children exhibit too much affection to the opposite sex in their company. Coupled with the fact that Aunt Bess was an upstanding, conventional, God-fearing human being, Merla knew the score.

Merla introduced him to Aunt Bess, Eddie, and Gloria.

Aunt Bess said, "I've heard so much about you. I'm so pleased to meet you although I wish the occasion were different. I think you are just as I would have imagined".

"I hope I haven't disappointed you. Pleased to meet you and I'm so sorry for your loss. We were coming to see you but it just means we are here earlier than expected and under difficult circumstances", replied Raymond with a warm, compassionate smile.

Anxiously Merla said, "Excuse me and sorry to interrupt, but can I have a look at the programme please. I know we can't do anything about it if there are typos or mistakes, but I need to put my mind at rest".

"I'm sure it will be OK darling, and if there are any typos, we can change them before the funeral. It'll be fine love, don't worry", he said reassuringly.

Jenny was pleased to see Raymond and they spend some time talking and playing while Merla checked the programme, putting her mind at rest. He was very tired but didn't show his tiredness as he was aware of how important it was to support Merla and her family. Food was an important part of showing hospitality and to keep her mind off her loss, Aunt Bess cooked a splendid welcoming dinner for Raymond. That evening after dinner, Raymond phoned for the same taxi driver Cedric, to take him and Merla to the hotel. Jenny stayed with Aunt Bess, Eddie, and Gloria. They would be hiring a car the next day while Raymond was there as it was frustrating waiting for a driver to pick them up and deliver them. Not only that, Raymond liked to be self-reliant when it came to going places, as he hated lateness. He also realised the importance of getting around in a new country and he was dubious about the standard of the taxi-drivers' driving. Not only did they drive recklessly, but also he doubted whether they had insurance cover. That night, the couple expressed how much they had missed each other, as if they had been apart for months!

On the morning of the funeral, the couple made their way to Aunt Bess in the hired car, setting off early to support Aunt Bess, as they knew it would be a difficult day for all concerned. Merla went over the Obituary, which she would be reading. Eddie and Gloria also went over the poem and reading they wrote especially for their father. Naturally, they were all nervous but

Merla tried to maintain composure by supporting the family.

The songs were moving and had most people in tears. When it was Merla's turn to read the obituary, she became very anxious and as she read, her voice kept breaking up; tears fell down her cheeks towards the end but she delivered the piece with poise, confidence and dignity. The hardest part for all of the family was when they went to the burial ground and the coffin was lowered in the ground, and the gravediggers, together with all the men folks, covered the coffin with earth, Aunt Bess, Merla and the family wept inconsolably. Crying released all the tension they felt since hearing the news; it was quite cathartic. Prior to the burial, they held themselves together by organising the event and now it was happening, outbursts of emotions flowed unreservedly.

The next day they spent with Aunt Bess and the family. After the tension of the preparation, yesterday's service, it was a relief to have an easy relaxed day. Aunt Bess looked at Merla's engagement ring and asked about the wedding. They told her about the house they were buying and hoped to complete the transaction when they returned. The wedding was on the card for next year but they didn't yet have a date.

Merla was more interested into how they were going to cope now the main breadwinner was no longer with them. Bess never really had to look after the bills but since Harry's first illness, she has been taking care of the finance. Both had small pensions and although Uncle Harry worked on the farm, he didn't earn a lot there. He rented out a large portion to a couple of farmers who paid him rent. The money they earned from the farm helped to supplement their income. He also sold food to people going to the market and although this was nominal, he did bring home a lot of the food he cultivated. Merla looked at the breakdown of their spending and agreed she would send them some money every month to assist. She also promised to buy credit for Eddie and Gloria's mobile phones which had become the new gizmo for young people. Aunt Bess had already lined up the man who helped Uncle Harry to work on the farm with the cultivation. She knew how people behaved in the country so would keep an eye on the situation and review it weekly. Scrutinising the weekly and monthly outgoings Merla wondered if savings on the household bills were possible.

One thing that stood out conspicuously was employing a weekly helper.

"You don't need her Auntie - this is unnecessary. Get Eddie and Gloria to help with the cleaning. They are big and need to start helping with the housework. It will teach them to be responsible. I'll have a word with them", said Merla.

The next day she and Raymond took Jenny, Eddie, and Gloria to the beach. This gave them a break from all that had happened and it gave Eddie and Gloria a chance to relax after their loss. The pair was aware they only had a few days left after helping to sort out the insurance documents and everything official that was bothering Aunt Bess. They briefed Eddie and Gloria as to what was outstanding and needed doing. They also stacked the fridge and cupboards with lots of food and the last day they spent packing and relaxing with the family. It was not a holiday so although they got some rest, it was a difficult time.

The return day was now here. Filled with sadness they bid farewell to Aunt Bess, Eddie, and Gloria. Raymond negotiated the bends carefully as he drove the hired car slowly down the hill. Car horns blew at him for going too slowly. He told himself that he had not had an accident since he has been there, even although the other drivers used the roads as racing tracks, and he wasn't going to have one on his return day.

The taxis lined the road leading to the airport entrance. Raymond returned the hired car and was pleasantly surprised they didn't find anything wrong with it. The airport was packed. People's suitcases bulged precariously as if they were going to burst open suddenly. Over-enthusiastic airport officials officiously and diligently weighed the suitcases and took pleasure in announcing they were over the authorized weight. Cynics were well aware of their intentions: They took pleasure in charging extra for overweight bags, even going over by an ounce, as they were jealous - jealous that they were staying and the holiday makers were leaving. It's as if the last day was their final chance to put a spanner in the works to spoil any happy memories the holidaymakers might have had during their stay.

After checking in, Merla, Raymond and Jenny sat down with their hand luggage and did some people watching. Straw hats bought at the craft markets adorned heads. The wearers being fully aware that once they returned home those hats were redundant, as they were incongruous in a cold dreary climate. Women were shouting at the flight attendants behind the desk making sure everyone was aware of their anger and frustration. "I'm not taking any more out of that case!" "I'm not paying any extra as that is what I brought and they didn't charge me any extra when I was leaving!" "I've already put some in the other case!" "You're all a bunch of bloody thieves"! Anger got the better of some of the passengers but the attendants just dug their heels in even more, stoically determined to prove who were in charge.

They boarded the plane on time and it wasn't long before they were off. Luckily for them they all sat together on the right hand side of the aisle with three seats. With Jenny taking the window seat, it wasn't long before she fell asleep. Merla and Raymond shared jokes, conversed, but with underlying sadness for their loss. They tried to watch a film, but Merla struggled to watch the entire film as she kept looking at everyone that walked down the aisle, checking on Jenny and eventually reading. After a nap, which wasn't truly a nap as they just closed their eyes, the plane landed early in the morning the next day. The taxi driver picked them up and dropped off Raymond first as he was closer to the airport and then Merla and Jenny. The couple parted with a kiss and promised to ring each other later on in the day. Tiredness and jet lag determined the rest of the day, with only a short call to Aunt Bess to say they had arrived safely back and Mrs. G getting a cursory call, but with the promise that Merla would call later in the week.

The weekend flew by quickly and already they were preparing to return to work and school on the Monday morning. The next thing they checked on was how the house purchasing was going, not that they expected much to change during their time away. Their main concern was that they weren't gazumped especially while they were absent. This was not supposed to happen legally, but unofficially it does. That was one of the reasons Raymond did not want to get too excited about the house. They didn't take any photographs of the place as again it seemed like tempting providence, but was now keen to take another look at the property.

"Darling I was thinking of all of us going away for Christmas, just a long weekend, somewhere warm, maybe in Spain perhaps. What do you think?" asked Raymond.

She replied, "Great idea but I would rather sort out the house-buying and selling my place first; and getting to grips with our wedding finance, before incurring any further expenses", said Merla, in her usual practical voice. "However if you think it will be an inexpensive do-able holiday, I'm for it. You are good at costing, so I'll leave it to you. Remember I have to help Aunt Bess now. I would also just feel more comfortable selling this place first. I don't want you to think I'm a stick in the mud".

"Look love, I think you are. We are getting that time off anyway so it wouldn't impinge on our time. I just feel we need to recharge our batteries and a change of environment wouldn't do us any harm. I think it can be done cheaply. We don't have to book a five-star hotel and there are lots of cheaper flights going out from the smaller airports even at that time of the year".

It may have irked him slightly that he had to justify a holiday, so he casually said, "When we next meet up, let's have a chat about how we see our future relationship, our plans, what irks us and what and where we would like to do together. It's also important that we start on the right footing, listening and communicating. Please think about it and write everything down so we can know how to please each other as a lot of relationships falter because the other person isn't listening and may be taking the partner for granted", Raymond said in a serious but loving manner.

"Don't you think it's highly unromantic? I love you with all your faults and I hope you feel the same way also. Suppose I don't like what you like, I don't want what you want. Where do we go from there? How many couples do this Raymond? Surely we can work it out as we go along?"

"You hit the nail on the head. I love you also with all your foibles, as that can be endearing; and we are not going to be the same and think the same, but we need to discuss and compromise so there is no resentment in our relationship. Some couples don't know what their partner wants. A lot of divorce could have been avoided if they didn't allow resentment to build up over months/ years. It's all to do with give and take and compromising and generally communicating. Don't you think? We are going into a relationship, which we are going to make endure for a lifetime so I think we should aim for the best there is in our relationship. I really want us to be happy and contented with each other".

"I think compromising as we go along is better. I agree with you that we should listen and take on board the others feelings, but still think it's not a shopping list and we may not know what we want in a relationship at this time in our lives, or we might change our minds at 40 or later. It's all about compromising and listening to the other person."

"True and I agree with what you say but we will grow together and change together; we can just say what we need now at this time in our lives. Do you know that some people see a marriage counsellor before marriage? I think it's the sensible thing to do because when I marry you, it's for life. I want us to be happy, to be so close; we become a couple, but also with the freedom to be individuals. I wouldn't want you to lose your personality, but neither do I want the relationship to fail," he said with a smile.

"OK Mister. How and why did we get on to this conversation?"

"It came up because I don't think you realised how important it is for me that we travel as much as possible during our marriage", said Raymond. "I've already travelled to several countries but want to continue to do so with my wife, and children.

"It makes sense; I really didn't know that travelling was so important to you. It's **not** important to me but I can easily live with that compromise!" she said laughing.

"Anyway I should have asked you - how are you today? How was work? How is Jenny?" asked Raymond.

"Busy, busy; the usual passing back to me and updating me as to what was done with my files and what I need to do. Jenny was excited to get back to school to see her friends. The estate agent rang to say they would like to do a block booking on the flat on Saturday, which suits me just fine. I think we are going to go for just block booking. Hate people traipsing through the place in drips and drab. We can meet for lunch while they are there if you want and I will bring my list."

"OK agreed lets go to the Shopping Centre on Saturday around 12.30", he replied.

On entering the car park, it was nearly full and they had completely forgotten how at that time of the day it was like a heavy-duty magnet, dragging cars to the shops. Both had their lists and promised once the discussion was over, they would swap lists so they could remember what the other liked.

The eating areas were not private so it was difficult to exchange their views openly but they managed to speak quietly, while they waited for their food to arrive.

Both wanted to have an honest, open relationship, where they discussed together finance and planned the major issues in their relationship. Paradoxically, they also wanted a degree of independence and individuality.

Raymond wanted to travel; he hated shopping especially for clothes. He hated banality in any form and needed a partner he could converse with at all times. He liked strong women but who behaved in a feminine but confident manner; he disliked obesity in both men and women; he hated untidiness especially in shared space. He was happy to share housework and the cooking, but would struggle if he were doing all the work while his partner was doing nothing. He hated lateness in all forms, but if unavoidable he wanted to be told in advance. He wanted a wife who shared his religious beliefs. Generally to give and take and understand the other person's feelings.

Merla wanted Raymond to treat and love Jenny like his own child. She wanted her husband to be loving and kind; loyal and faithful; to be ambitious and driven. To share the pain as well as the fun times; to be understanding if she was tired and didn't feel like lovemaking. To be a true friend so she can talk to him about anything, in a civil manner, not domineering, shouting, or bullying. She didn't mind if he was a little untidy, but would not be cleaning up after her husband. She would like a partner who supported her endeavours and ambitions, and especially her personal goals. She certainly didn't want a penny-pincher, where she needed to account for every penny she spent. She would like one night a month where they went out on their own as a couple.

"I think our likes, dislikes, and values are similar and some overlap so there are no major shocks here. As the saying goes, 'We are singing from the same hymn sheet'. "I promise to love Jenny as if she was my daughter. Here is my list for your retention," said Raymond formally, but jokingly.

"Here is mine. Yes, our values are similar and I promise to love you. We should remember from today what we promised each other." she sealed with a kiss.

The food had now arrived, Jenny put her book and game away, and they tucked in happily, finishing with coffee and water. The couple now spent the rest of the afternoon, talking to Jenny and giving her their undivided attention. At the end of the meal, the agent rang to say they had received an offer, which was £10K less than the asking price. They agreed to a compromise of a £5K reduction. Merla asked the agent to leave the flat on the market just in case the sale was aborted. As far as they were aware, the sale of the flat was going through but of course, nothing was certain until the buyer signed on the dotted line.

As Christmas approached, Raymond's Christmas present to them was a trip to Barcelona, Spain. He was in the initial stage of learning Spanish and wanted to go somewhere in Spain to practise the language (albeit briefly), so this present wasn't strictly altruistic. It wasn't his first trip to Spain; in fact, Raymond had been three times before. The places already visited were Madrid, Granada, and Seville. The hotel was a taxi drive from the airport, so there wouldn't be any gruelling travel and it would mean they could just hop on the train from their end. Merla was now looking forward to this trip as neither she nor Jenny had ever been to Spain before. As Christmas approached, she packed the presents in the suitcase and ensured she made her must-have Christmas cake. She also always made a cake for Mrs. Green. She wasn't a great cook but she certainly could bake a mean cake and played to her strengths. Merla was happy to sit back and let Raymond take charge of the travel itinerary.

Barcelona, the cosmopolitan capital of Spain's Catalonia region, was a place he had read about in books. Its distinctive quirky art and Gothic architecture by Antoni Gaudi, appealed to him, as they were so different. The hotel was just off La Rambla, a beautiful vibrant tree-lined street with flower stalls, a market where the fresh gigantic mangos piled mountainously high, and several restaurants just waiting for tourists to enter. He also wanted to take them to the Sagrada Familia and La Pedrera. The photographs he had seen of La Pedrera housed beautiful Art Deco carved furniture. The quality of the workmanship reminded him of a bygone era, where beauty and quality went hand in hand. If time allowed, he also wanted to go to Park Guell. He knew he would not see all he wanted to show them in four days and was looking at this visit as a taster. In particular, he knew he wouldn't get time to go to the Picasso Museum. They ensured they took appropriate clothes as the weather varied while they were there, and although not t-shirt or beach weather, it was generally warm enough for just a jacket.

On visiting Sagrada Familia, she could see that Gaudi was a man of spiritual convictions. In 1883 Gaudi took over the design of the **Sagrada Familia**, transforming it into its Gothic and Art Nouveau forms. He devoted his last years to the project but at the time of his death in 1926 only a quarter of the project was complete. The Spanish Civil War interrupted its progress and relying on private donations hindered its completion which was now anticipated to be in 2026! However the progress made so far was impressive and tourists could see clearly how spectacular this Basilica would be once completed.

Merla said to Raymond, "How ironic that this man who spent his whole life working on these ambitious buildings and artwork, being ridiculed, should die not knowing the impact his designs would have on Barcelona, attracting so many tourists, earning revenue and providing jobs for its people. This one person was instrumental in making modern Barcelona what it is today. Life is so strange".

"A classic example of a person who believed in what he was doing. He had the conviction to continue regardless of criticisms and denunciation. He was definitely an independent thinker who continued regardless of ridicule", replied Raymond.

Jenny really loved the imaginative forms of the sculptures and colourful tiles Gaudi used in his work. She promised her mum she would be drawing and colouring tiles in that style and vibrancy when she returned home.

As expected, they didn't get to see all that Raymond wanted to show them as Christmas and Boxing Day got in the way with most shops and museums closed. Although they enjoyed the Christmas in Spain, the time went quickly and as such, it wasn't restful but enjoyable. Merla realised the effort Raymond had put into planning the short trip for herself and Jenny so she thought the present was original and thoughtful.

Their plans for the sale of the flat, and Merla and Jenny moving into a house were proceeding as planned. The flat sale and purchase of the house had now happened. The house and Raymond's flat would be in both names, and some of the proceeds from the sale of the flat used as a deposit for the house and on the wedding. They would save some of the money, but the house needed renovating and so they also needed to consider this. Just as well, the couple was also saving separately. They agreed to a date of 7 July for their wedding, which would take place at Raymond's church. They had also provisionally booked a local hotel for the reception. The wedding would be intimate and understated, as they couldn't stand the idea of an extravagant wedding when the money could be used on their honeymoon, and saving for their future.

Both mother and daughter started to de-clutter and box up the stuff they weren't taking. In the chaos, Jenny continued to practice her eleven plus papers, and Merla's workload increased: as Cyril became more confident in her ability, he gave her more complex files to work on. Life continued to progress steadily and as the weeks and months went by, the house move was now imminent. They agreed to exchange contracts in the first week in March. Merla employed builders so she could renovate the house before the wedding. With Raymond working long hours, he wouldn't be able to decorate before the wedding, plus Merla wanted it all done professionally and as speedily as possible. The invitation would be going out three months before to Aunt Bess, Mrs Green, and other guests including her boss, Cyril and his wife, and a few other friends plus Raymond's family and friends. The guest list was average because of the amount of people Raymond knew. They were determined to have a decent wine list and quality food for the foodies.

Finding a reputable builder who was prepared to start soon was difficult. The one they found agreed to buy many of the materials from where he traded and therefore he knew what materials were available. On top of that, the builder could provide swatches and colour charts to show the couple. Getting the goods at trade price allowed the builder to add on extra, but this was still more competitive than buying from a retail outlet.

The day of the move was inevitably hectic. Stupidly they had omitted to put on the boxes the designated rooms or content, and with just a number on each box, they had to open each box before it revealed where things should go. The removal men just offloaded the boxes in each room. A big mistake but this was a learning curve for when and if they moved again. Its only when one is moving the extent to what one has acquired is identified. Merla was shocked at the number of things she had accumulated over a relatively short period.

The builders started working before all the boxes were unpacked. They stuck to their schedule and worked to a deadline. Thus far, the couple were satisfied with the workmanship and the builders worked cleanly and professionally. In between sorting out the house, she had to buy her wedding dress, sort out Jenny and Gloria's bridesmaid dresses and that of the maid of honour, which would probably be Ruth. Probably, as she had not asked her as yet. Merla wasn't sure if Raymond's sister or any of his family would want to be a bridesmaid. To save time, she was also going to buy Aunt Bess' suit, subject to checking beforehand the colour and style she preferred. Merla would also be making the cake and getting the shop to decorate it, as she was not great at cake decorating. The couple couldn't decide what song they should play for their first dance: "So Amazing" by Luther Vandross or "At Last" by Etta James. These songs were sentimental and mushy but they loved both.

Time was now moving on for the wedding day. Seventy guests received invitations. Aunt Bess got visas for herself, Gloria and Eddie. They would be staying for a month as they were going to look after Jenny when the couple went on their honeymoon. The food would be West Indian cuisine, with rum punch and wine flowing freely. The caterers were already booked, also all the wedding necessities such as cars and flowers. The bride chose plain cream raw silk for her dress with a long veil, understated but long enough to cover the dress. The colour for the maid of honour and bridesmaid's dress was yet undecided but they were likely to be soft pastel shades.

It was such a shame that Uncle Harry was not around to give her away, but Merla would not be making any effort to contact her natural father, who hadn't been a part of her life since her mother died. Even if he lived next door to her, she would not want him at her wedding, as there was still unfinished business between them. He would definitely spoil her day. Merla asked Monty to give her away to which he was very happy to oblige. "I didn't have a natural father when I was a young girl and young adult, so I can certainly do without him now - bastard!" she said to herself.

After her mother died, her father lost contact with the family when he moved away and did not make any effort to stay in touch or to help support Merla. This still angered her and she saw Aunt Bess and Uncle Harry as her real parents. There was no excuse on his part, as they never moved anywhere. If he wanted to, she believed he could have found her. She didn't know if he was dead or alive and she didn't care.

As the weeks approached, Jenny got more and more excited; this would be the first time she was a bridesmaid. The couple met regularly to exchange news and ensure everything was in order. Merla met Raymond's parents a couple more times but spoke on the phone regularly to keep them in the loop and make them feel included in the forthcoming event. Raymond also moved his belongings into his new home, leaving the essentials at his flat. He sorted out the honeymoon, which would be a surprise for Merla. The only clues were she needed her passport, and it was going to be hot, so she needed swimsuit, and summer clothes. Aunt Bess had now arrived and helped Merla to sort out the house. The couple met on the Wednesday before the wedding day to dine out on their own.

"I just wanted to meet you alone to have a chat," said Raymond. "Are you sure you want to get married, or rather lets rephrase that, do you want to marry me? I don't have any doubt in my mind that you are the one for me, and I would love you to be my wife".

"I want you as my husband and I have no doubt in my mind we can make it work as we are going into this commitment with our eyes wide open," replied Merla.

"Let's pray for God's blessings on our decision; let's ask Him to guide and protect us as we start our new life together", said Raymond.

Whilst waiting for their food to arrive, they prayed openly but quietly for God's blessings, in the dimly-lit restaurant. This behaviour was completely alien to Merla to be praying in public, but she went along with it as Raymond was at ease with this custom. They would not be seeing each other until their wedding day on Saturday.

As they kissed goodnight, Raymond said, "Even though it's a bride's prerogative, please don't be late. You know what a stickler I am for time keeping. I know you are going to look gorgeous on your day. Speak to you tomorrow love".

The night before the wedding Merla didn't sleep properly as she was thinking about the day, so she woke exceptionally early.

"Thank God for make-up!" she shouted to Aunt Bess. "I didn't get much sleep last night at all. I just kept thinking about the day and hoping everything will run smoothly".

Aunt Bess said reassuringly, "You'll be fine. Everything will be fine. Your face does not need too much make-up. You're beautiful as is".

"Thanks but I don't believe you. I will take your compliment and run with it anyway. You know me, I like everything to run smoothly. I cannot stand when plans go wrong especially on such an occasion as my wedding. When so much thought has gone into the event, I want it to work".

Merla looked at her spreadsheet to reassure herself that everything was in place. Aunt Bess made cornmeal porridge - a staple breakfast for everyone, as it was going to be a long day and there was uncertainty as to when they would next eat. Aunt Bess felt it was a sustaining, nourishing meal for that day. Merla ate only some of hers, as she was now getting nervous, although this was not outwardly noticeable. She rang all the relevant people, to make sure everything was in order. Ruth arrived early to get dressed with the women. She brought with her 'something borrowed' for Merla to wear. A beautiful gold bracelet Monty gave her on one of their anniversaries. The hairdresser arrived, then the bouquets. When she put on the cream silk wedding dress, with pearl necklace and earrings, the bride looked stunning. Her hair pinned up to accommodate the two-tier veil, which was plain and long. They were now all ready and Monty came dressed to accompany Merla down the aisle. Mrs Green would be travelling with Aunt Bess, Jenny, and Ruth in the second car, while Merla and Monty travelled in the bridal car.

With tears in her eyes, Aunt Bess said, "You look beautiful".

The reception room was close to the church so it was easier for Raymond to oversee the reception event. He, his family, and friends had sorted out the music, ensured the tables laid specifically to Merla's request, and checked that the hotel had sorted out the food. As he waited for her to arrive, his best man reassured him, he had the rings.

The wedding march played and Merla coolly sauntered down the aisle with Monty by her side. She promised herself she would not cry as her tears would *disturb* her make-up but she was inwardly emotional as she approached her soon-to-be husband.

He whispered in her ears, "You look absolutely beautiful Mrs Wilson".

She answered demurely with a smile.

The front of the church, probably built around the 1930s, made of terracotta bricks, was simple and unadorned. It was only when visitors approached the entrance doors were they aware that it was indeed a church as through the internal glass windows was an impressive cross adorning the church altar. On the rectangular table were leaflets of past and forthcoming events and the order of the wedding service. The interior, a little austere, could easily have been mistaken for a Quaker or a Shaker meeting room. The organist played Wagner's "Bridal Chorus" with vigour as she walked down the aisle. People glanced round to see the bride. The couple chose hymns that most people knew so the energy in the church was infectious. They added personal messages to each other's vows as the minister went through the wedding vows. It was a lovely wedding ceremony - simple, personal, and intimate. As the ceremony ended, the bride and groom emerged from the church, smiling happily. Guests showered them with rice grain. The reception, held in a nearby hotel with the garden extending on to a park, had beautiful flowerbeds and a water lily pond. Photographers, both the professional and amateurs, waited patiently to capture the moment. As the bride and groom entered the hotel reception, waiting hotel staff greeted guests with glasses of wine and other drinks. Hors d'oeuvres followed. The schedule was on time. As guests found their tables, they sat down to eat. The chef specialised in Caribbean food and therefore the salt fish fritters and avocado slice as starter, followed by jerk chicken and vegetarian dishes as the main meal, were original and tasty. A box housed the greeting cards and a major department store delivered the presents from guests. Merla had made the fruitcake, but the local cake shop decorated expertly and it looked professional and creative. Orchids and flowers made out of icing, delicately adorn the cake. There were no bride and groom figures on the top of the cake as requested by Merla. She introduced Raymond to Cyril and his wife. Cyril wished them a wonderful future together and remarked to his wife how they appeared well suited and happy together.

Wonderful speeches followed the meal. One of Raymond's friends was the Master of Ceremony and as he knew Raymond from a long way back, he was able to throw in a few anecdotes in his speech. He controlled the entire evening, making sure speeches did not overrun. Their opening dance was to Luther Vandross', 'So Amazing'. Other guests then joined on the dance floor. Food and drinks flowed freely and guests danced and laughed the night away. Although the reception finished quite late, the couple left before it ended to start their honeymoon. They stayed in the hotel, in the honeymoon suite that night. Their close friends and relations took care of the closing section, ensuring the left over wedding cake, food and the cards were sent to the couple's house.

Merla had tried in vain to get from Raymond their honeymoon destination but without any success. Again, it was a new thing for her to rely on someone else to take charge. On the flip-side, she liked the idea of a surprise.

The next day in the afternoon, they returned to their home as Mr and Mrs Wilson, full of joy and still ecstatic about their wedding the previous day. They looked through their cards and presents, had dinner with the family and Mrs Green. Raymond checked over their holiday papers, as the taxi would be collecting them the next morning. Raymond made sure he packed his own suitcase, as he did not want to give any clues to Merla. He packed a roll of toilet paper in his luggage; an odd thing to pack but someone had told him there might be a shortage of toilet paper in Cuba as tourists were restricted to only about two sheets when they went on excursions and needed to visit a toilet! He chuckled to himself as he was going to pack two rolls of toilet papers. However, when he thought what the customs people may be thinking when they searched his luggage, he opted for one roll.

The secret was shattered and the penny had now dropped when the checking-in clerk said to Raymond, "Have you been to Havana before?" Merla tried in vain to pretend she didn't hear that question but then the checking-in clerk repeated the same question to Merla.

After all the effort Raymond made, was clearly irritated by this question. He said to Merla, "That was such an irrelevant question. If she wanted to be friendly, why couldn't she think of another question? I already put the name of the hotel on the tags. Why did she need to know if we've been to Cuba before?" He pondered about saying something to her about how she had ruined the surprise but he went through security without commenting.

"Sweetheart, I am so pleased with your choice. It is still a surprise and you couldn't have picked a better place. I've always wanted to go to Cuba! I'm really looking forward to this! Thank you! You're a star, Raymond! In normal circumstances, you wouldn't have minded her question - would you? I'm sure she was just being friendly" she reassured him with a kiss.

The flight landed in the early evening in Havana and highly organised drivers in their vintage cars waited outside the airport for passengers to select their car. As the couple came off the plane, their immediate impression was how different the country was; it was like stepping back in time to the 1950s with the vintage Oldsmobiles, Chevrolets, Buicks, and the old Plymouths. Normally displayed in museums, they couldn't help but admire the beautiful classic cars, parked in rows, waiting for the tourists. They felt as if they were observing a free vintage car show, usually frequented by car enthusiasts. The exterior of the cars were sparklingly clean and well cared for, although inside the upholstery was more unforgiving with shabby leather seats worn away, but that was not surprising for their age.

Arriving at the Hotel Republique in Havana, the couple phoned and informed Aunt Bess they had arrived safely. Then they unpacked, showered, made passionate love and had a rest. After getting up, they decided to venture out to survey their environment.

Havana at night has a diverse setting. She moves to the sound of the Bantu beats, the Spanish guitar, and sad love songs. Open air patios, leading to restaurants and cocktail bars, where tourists drank rum and cocktails alfresco, while they listened or danced to the salsa and rumba beats set the scene for a lively fun holiday for the couple.

Already Raymond had planned their itinerary to get maximum benefit from their holiday. This suited Merla, as she did not know where she was going, and she wouldn't have had the time to plan anyway. Like the start of her marriage to Raymond, she was enjoying this early stage of the unknown journey.

The hotel room was spacious, clean, and comparatively modern, with western facilities such as large mirrors, king sized beds and mixer taps in the bathroom, juxtaposed against the outside buildings, with shabby dated exterior and where time stood still in the 1950s.

While in bed, Raymond said to her, "Sweetheart, I have planned a provisional itinerary I think you should like, but if you want to go any other places not listed, we can do that as well or make some adjustment".

The biggest bugbear already noticeable was the lack of internet connection in Cuba, even in their modern hotel. The hotel receptionists were quite nonchalant about what they perceived as a Western phenomenon of always having access to the internet. "You're on holiday, why do you want the internet anyway? You should just enjoy yourself. Relax!"

Raymond said to his wife sarcastically, "How thoughtful of them to be considering the tourists or are they keeping the internet from the people in case it corrupts them? The genie is already out of the bottle, people! Good job I had the foresight to print out this information before leaving".

"These things are trivial love, and they are not going to stop us from having a great holiday. Let's get an early night as we are going to have a busy day tomorrow", Merla reassured him. "You and I know that the internet has its advantages and disadvantages. We lived without it before and it's not good to rely on anything or anybody completely.

The next day they got up early for touring Old Havana. At breakfast, the food was surprisingly familiar with smatterings of Cuban cuisine. There was choripan, which was a Cuban bread with thinly cut Spanish chorizo sausages, fried plantains, thick slices of ham and of course omelettes made to the customers' preference. Exotic fruit juices such as sour sop and jackfruit juices were on display to tempt the adventurous holidaymaker. These exotic drinks were not exactly unfamiliar to the couple as they were grown in the Caribbean. They ate enough breakfast to ward off any hunger pangs until dinnertime. What was interesting at the buffet tables were Cuban families, probably fairly affluent families, were either staying at the hotel or used the hotel as a restaurant.

"This is what I had in mind for us to do today." Raymond showed her the photographs from the guidebook.

"As they're more or less in the same vicinity we could visit these sites today. Catedral de La Habana, Calle Mercaderes, Plaza Vieja, Museo de la Revolucion and if we are not too tired the Museo National de Bellas Artes".

"I think we should visit the museums first and if we have time, we see the others. Also after walking around the museums we may want to do the others another day as we may be too tired. The Museo de la Revolucion was one place I wanted to see as I have heard about this and it's obviously an important place, outlining the revolutionary process," said Merla, having studied the guide.

"OK Mrs Wilson" he replied with a smile. "We are also going to Varadero for four days so we should have enough time to see all we need to in Havana. Hope you have carried your swimsuits, for Varadero," he added with another smile.

The day went off really well, but they weren't used to walking in the heat. Everything was highly organised. Outside the hotel were taxicabs and the Transgaviota coach, which took tourists to their destinations. On their way to The Museo de la Revolucion, they passed beautiful buildings, left untouched from the 1950s, but on closer inspection, were crumbling and dilapidated and there was an urge to ask 'What are they doing to protect and stop this decay?' In between buildings, they met the locals selling their wares on the side-walk, but unlike some of the other countries where tourists were forced to purchase what they didn't want, Cuba was different, and the tourists didn't feel pressurised to buy anything. They were more subtle.

Merla remarked "I notice that the people although most are poor, they preferred to sell something instead of begging; they were dignified and had a stoic, proud demeanour".

Raymond remarked, "But you don't know if it's the Government who are suppressing their behaviour or if it's genuine that they are a proud nation. The government is very strict when it comes to showing the country in a positive light. There are undercover people policing the country and we may not know them but the ordinary Cubans know who they are. It's a bit like a sixth sense I suppose".

"I believe it's the latter. You can suppress individuals but surely you cannot repress a whole nation indefinitely?" replied Merla.

"Really? My dear there are several ways the mass can be suppressed without even realising it. Germany under Hitler is a good example. Remember all of Fidel's and Guevara's ideas were revolutionary. That included indoctrinating or *re-educating* the whole population subliminally or obviously and if that didn't work, the next step was conformity and compliance; I presume indelibly ingrained in the entire structure of society. That must have been one hell of a job to change the entire society's thinking, especially as the Americans were so influential in the country and people aspired to that lifestyle. When one thinks about it, these revolutionaries were brave but its telling what is possible when human beings feel strongly about their liberty. Those who were determined not to conform or could afford to leave, left".

What was revealing about The Revolucion Museum was how well planned this Revolution was and fascinating how they captured the period and showed the process of the Revolution.

"I don't know what I expected to see but I certainly didn't realise pre-Revolution the country was as corrupt and known as the island of sin, with the society consumed by gambling, the Mafia, drugs, and prostitution. How Fulgencio Batista, the then elected President of Cuba and his cronies, were working together with the American Mafiosi to siphon off Cuban state funds to build hotels and casinos. No wonder there was a revolution!" said Merla.

"But you have to remember not all Cubans were for the Revolution. You just have to look at America, and particularly Miami, there are many Cubans living there. The ruling class was against the sudden changes that took place, as it would obviously affect their lifestyle and they didn't want to live like the Russians. To them that was a retrograde move. Like all human beings, you support what is going to enhance and benefit your family's future; paradoxically the poor had nothing to lose", said Raymond.

They visited first The Revolucion Museum and as they were close by, the couple then went to the Museo National de Bellas Artes, which boasts ancient Egyptian, Greek and Roman art and European masters with several Cuban artists' work. A noticeable difference was the way art was made from recycled materials: nothing seemed to be wasted. Such was their creativity that the lack of materials didn't get in their way for making art. *Necessity is the mother of invention* definitely applied here.

"It reminds me of how Picasso and other artists had to work with recycled materials during the Second World War when material was scarce. Some of their art reminds me of Duchamp's *ready-mades*", said Raymond.

"What do you mean *ready-mades* and how comes you know so much about this?" asked Merla.

"I did a short course on Art Appreciation because of my interest in the subject. Marcel Duchamp was part of the Cubist, Dadaist, and Conceptual art movements and he coined the phrase *ready-mades,* as he used ordinary, maybe found, objects to create art. He used a urinal as a sculptural piece of art naming it "*Fountain*" and he got away with it. He also mounted a bicycle on the wall and displayed it as an artwork. Surprisingly when mounted on the wall, it became a sculptural piece. Picasso did several sculptural pieces with found materials, as art materials were scarce during 2nd World War. I suppose it is all about believing in your art and yourself no matter what the circumstances and also taking the mickey out of pretentious art. I must admit I don't understand it all but some of it I like."

"I find it fascinating. I like the way they used the barbed wire as a frame to, I suppose, reinforce the message of hardship in a piece of artwork," added Merla.

The day went well and when they got home were so tired, just had time to shower and go for dinner.

The next day after breakfast, they walked around Old Havana and then they headed for the Plaza de la Catedral and had a drink at the Ernest Hemingway's favourite place La Bodeguita del Medio.

"Everything seems so different, I am sure we can take more photographs down those quaint alleyways. Look at the murals on the buildings down that alleyway!" said Merla excitedly. What was surprising for the couple was how much the Cubans loved public art.

The next day they had a ride in an open top Chevrolet vintage car. The driver could speak perfect English and doubled up as a guide, taking them around places like the Plaza de la Revolucion where a portrait of Che Guevara adorns the façade of the Minister of the Interior.

The evening was spent at the Rumba del Callejon de Hamel. The rumba music was so infectious Merla couldn't wait to get on the dance floor. She hardly ever danced but she threw caution to the wind as she was anonymous in a foreign country so didn't care if she looked ridiculous or not. Eventually she convinced Raymond to dance; he was a little hesitant and reserved but with a couple more pina coladas, he was more relaxed and really enjoyed dancing.

The week was going fast and they covered the tourists' areas including the last evening attending a Buena Vista Social Club show. Although they came too far not to attend this show, they found it commercial and lacking spontaneity. Most dancers/singers were on automatic pilot and so the show felt stilted as if they were just going through the motions.

The next day they travelled on a special coach to Varadero. Another thing they noticed was how highly intelligent the guides and all those working in the tourists industry were. This guide on the bus was a professor in a university. Apparently, most of the highly skilled people earned more money working with tourists than working in their academic field. The journey seemed long as they cleverly took detours to a cave, a stall selling pina colada and food; plus the obligatory cigar factory to buy cigars and bottles of rum. Before long the tourists had bought things they never even considered before. This was good business acumen as everybody bought cigars and rum and that was likely the only way the tourists would have seen and bought these items. After all, the ordinary country folk needed to earn a living.

The beach at Varadero was nearly always empty, considering it was a tourist resort but that suited the couple just fine. Every day they swam, they read, they talked intimately and danced in the evening as the music blasted on the beach. The pina-coladas flowed freely from a pop-up bar on the beach. The couple learned to dance the samba and rumba or at least that is what they thought, but they promised to continue the learning on their return home, as they loved the freedom of the dance movements; it was almost cathartic.

The picture postcard beach was usually empty or with very few people. This could have something to do with the time of year, but Raymond doubted that. There were several beaches: white sand and blue sky, and blue sea. The people were highly organised so those who wanted to tour other areas could do so without having to lie on a beach. They played to their past criminal history. The couple visited a restaurant, purportedly used by Al Capone. By the end of the four days lying on the beach, they were ready to go home. The last days of their holiday, they spent on the beach resting, swimming, dancing, drinking, and reading.

The exact coach that took them brought them back to Havana. It was unusual as coaches collected and delivered tourists to and from Varadero and there was no guarantee if you would see the same driver. Returning to the Jose Marti Airport in Havana, this was the first time they experienced chaos. The queue zigzagged in the airport reception area and stretched round the corner of the entrance. It seemed to take forever to check in and the heat didn't help either. The couple went straight up to the first-class check-in desk and upgraded their flight, so they didn't have to queue. This was a relief as they were tired travelling from Varadero. In the first class lounge, they sank into a leather sofa with cold drinks in their hands.

As the plane took off, Merla said to her husband, "I am so pleased we upgraded to first class. Now I know why travellers pay the extra for first class. The seats are so spacious and comfortable not to mention the food, which is so much nicer and served on plates. Thank you so much for a wonderful holiday …sorry honeymoon".

"What I liked was we didn't have to wait long in that horrendous queue in the heat," said Raymond, as they arrived home. For the first time they were going to live as man and wife.

CHAPTER 5

Jenny was ecstatic to see her mum and stepdad; so were Aunt Bess, Eddie, and Gloria. They spent the weekend enjoying family life although they were aware that Aunt Bess and her children would return home next week.

That night Merla and Raymond talked intimately in their bedroom after Merla spent some time with her daughter.

"I suppose we should have discussed this before but it's better late than never", Raymond said, "But how do you want me to treat Jenny?"

"How do you mean?"

"I want to start off on the right foot and for us to live together in harmony, so I need to know if there is anything I should or shouldn't do and say to Jenny. Can I reprimand her for example? What's not negotiable?"

"Well I don't know. We are all facing a new situation but I am sure if Jenny *feels* like she is a part of *both* our lives, everything will be fine, so treat her as you would your own child and she will respond accordingly. Like all parents, it's a learning process. We learn on the job, so don't worry. I never want either of you to feel tense about the relationship. It's all to do with trusting each other. If she has done something wrong, tell her off. Don't beat round the bush, but of course, I want her to be happy in your company. It's also about balance and her not feeling she is losing her mother I suppose. I would like her to call you dad as I feel we should be one family and she needs a father".

"OK that's fine by me. What about the home - are there any areas that I am not allowed to enter, like housework and cooking?"

"Of course not; whoever gets home first can start the dinner. If you are too tired and don't feel like helping to cook and tidy up, I will understand. Likewise, if I'm tired, I expect you to take up the reins. It's a matter of give and take, don't you think? If neither of us feels like cooking, we get a take-away!"

"Agree totally, although I am useless at ironing, but willing to learn", said Raymond.

On Monday, they took Aunt Bess, Eddie, and Gloria to the airport. As they said goodbye this time they cried, as they were uncertain as to when they would next meet. Poor Raymond looked on and tried to reassure the family they would of course meet again soon. Merla was also sad as she was already wondering how she was going to cope without that extra help, especially when she went back to work; not to mention that she would be missing the only relatives she had.

The first few days back at work was busy. She was even busier as she was now nearly in the middle of her training to become a solicitor.

She was late coming home, but Raymond left work on time so he picked up Jenny from Mrs. Green. They anticipated this outcome as leftovers from the day before was heated up for dinner.

Merla came in exhausted from the day's work. They ate the dinner Raymond heated up, in peace, but paused only to update each other on how the day had gone for everyone.

The next day was more or less a replica of the previous day, so Raymond collected Jenny but this time he prepared and cooked dinner. In bed, Raymond said, "How do you think I did with the dinner? I am just asking for feedback. I know I am not perfect, but don't want to disappoint you if I can help it".

Replying Merla said, "It was lovely darling but I don't expect you to be a chef as well! It's the first dinner you cooked for us anyway. It always tastes better when someone else cooks it anyway".

"Look babe, I want us to talk about anything that's bothering us and don't let things fester and once we have spoken, to take on board how the other person is feeling and try to sort it out" responded Raymond.

"I don't expect a perfect husband so stop it! Just relax!"

"I am not worried," said Raymond, "but it's important for us to talk and try to resolve issues as I know marriages that haven't lasted because the couple ignored concerns and then resentment build up in the relationship. If you hate the way I leave the bathroom, tell me, and vice versa; if I dislike your being late for any event, I will tell you, as these are issues that can be resolved and can make life so much more pleasant in the marriage".

Time had flown by quickly and before long, they fell into the routine of married life, and were planning Jenny's education. They wanted to give her the opportunity of having a grammar school education, as she was a bright child. In the evening, Jenny got homework and at weekends, she had extra lessons. Like most couples, they had their arguments but as agreed, they discussed and resolved as soon as there were disagreements. They had planned not to have any more children until she had become a solicitor and they were more financially secure. They anticipated another two years at the most for her studies if everything went as planned.

Jenny felt very secure with Raymond as her stepfather. He treated her like a daughter and felt their ready-made family was going well, although he wanted a child of his own at some point. Raymond had a couple of wage increases since their marriage and Merla's training was going well, so the couple was becoming more comfortable financially. All the DIY work that needed doing in the house was finished so they took the opportunity to go on holidays with Jenny or short breaks on their own. They were truly happy and content with their lives. In fact they were so happy, Merla, the pessimist, secretly kept wondering when her bubble was going to burst; she was more rational and less emotional. Raymond in his own way was far more romantic and idealistic.

Merla had stepped up on Jenny's eleven plus revisions, as that year she would be taking her exam. The after-school training was very intense as the date approached and the teacher had a high success rate. It was also about protecting her reputation as well, so she insisted on complete commitment by her students when they enrolled with her. Jenny worked hard and as expected, she passed her eleven plus. She got into the grammar school of Merla's choice. This was a big relief to all of them, as they did not want to pay school fees to a private school or send Jenny to the local comprehensive school, which did not have as good a reputation as the grammar school.

"Thank you so much for helping Jenny to pass her exam. I couldn't have done this without your help", said Merla to Raymond, sealing her words with a kiss.

That September Jenny started grammar school. Tears filled Merla's eyes as she dropped her off at school in her new school uniform. Time had flown so quickly, her baby was now at big school. Merla was also in her last year as a trainee solicitor.

"I am so sorry I am not spending sufficient time with you both, but you understand don't you?" said Merla to Raymond who was overseeing and helping Jenny with her schoolwork, to ensure she was on the right track with her work. After all, she was now at a school, which demanded higher academic results, and she had to assimilate into a new environment.

"Don't be silly love, we understand. I have explained things to Jenny and like every situation we face, we face them together and we don't want you to fail at the last hurdle. You have been doing so well you are nearly there," said Raymond.

"It's not like that love. When I do qualify, it does not mean that I will have less work. On the contrary, it's very likely I will have even more work!" said Merla.

"Like all hard-working couples we will cope; we will manage. Don't worry about it. I am so very proud of you and what you have done. You are our shining star." He said as he kissed her.

"Jen, how do you feel about mummy working so hard?" Merla asked, involving Jenny in the conversation.

Hesitating Jenny then answered, "You have always taught me to work hard mum and I see that is what you are doing, so I understand. I know you love us. In addition, I have dad if I need to know anything. I know you are always there for me, so don't worry mum".

"You are so grown up Jen since you started secondary school. You understand that we are working hard to make all our future lives better don't you?" asked Raymond.

"Yes I understand".

Merla and Raymond went into the bedroom for a brief moment and as they caressed each other, they vowed that they would all take a restful holiday when she finished her training.

Raymond was also active in the church and he assisted them where he could. He also loved this spiritual side of his life and both Merla and Jenny attended church with him whenever possible. It had become a part of their family schedule. Mrs Green sometimes went to church with them. She also sometimes invited them over for Sunday lunch and they did likewise. She had become a part of their extended family, and was supportive in all they did. They loved her and she still looked after Jenny when she finished school and during the holidays. She was a part of the family in every way.

Merla's last year of training was going well. Cyril, her mentor, was happy with her work. He was impressed with how she had doggedly progressed in her ambitious pursuits. He felt she was a doer, not someone who would waste his and her time.

They planned to have a child after she had qualified, as that would make her over 30. Jenny would be more self-sufficient at over14 years of age, and she would be able to help as a big sister. Whatever their plans she would be returning to work after maternity leave in any case. They hoped to hire a lived-in nanny to help with childcare and the housework but that was all in the future of course.

"We haven't had a cake for a long time. I am going to make us a mean meal and a cake this weekend". We have all worked so hard and I think we deserve to be spoiled with some good old-fashioned home-made carbohydrates! What do you think, should we include Mrs G?"

"Why not as long as it's not going to incur too much work for you," said Raymond. "I'll ask her when I collect Jenny tomorrow. Presumably you are having this dinner after church on Sunday".

The couple promised to enjoy their lives together and was aware that life had become too staid, if a little humdrum but promised each other this was a temporary situation. They would remind each other when this happened.

As weekend approached, Merla decided on the menu and insisted to Raymond that Mrs Green should not bring any food with her as she usually did.

"We can keep it simple with pumpkin soup for starter. I'm going to bake salmon, sweet potatoes, and vegetables - healthy main meal as we are having a piece of my cake for dessert."

"Sounds great darling", replied Raymond.

"When I qualify, we are going to have a big dinner for our friends and your family to celebrate. It's a long time since we had anyone round".

"Do you not mind all the work?" asked Raymond.

"Not at all - Love it! Plus the stress to qualify will be off me, so entertaining will be like a piece of cake."

On Sunday after church, Mrs Green returned with the family for dinner. It was wonderful having that extra person as it made them felt an extended family was with them and the conversation was relaxed and down to earth. Mrs Green was an intelligent woman who always brought another perspective to any discussion with her wealth of experience. While they ate, Merla shared their plans with Mrs Green. As Merla didn't now usually collect Jenny, they took the opportunity to also catch up on each others lives.

Mrs Green was very aware of how situations beyond their control could kibosh plans as she too had plans and wanted to share the future with her husband, who died prematurely, so sensitively and diplomatically she said. "I really love the way you guys are planning for your future, and it's important, but remember to enjoy life as you go along and please don't make your plans too rigid. You need to enjoy life now and stop postponing fun times."

The feedback from all the diners was the meal was delicious. Merla's cake also went down well as a dessert and she gave Mrs G the rest to take home. It was still very light outside so Mrs Green said she would walk off some of the food.

"If you don't take it, I'll eat it as Jenny and Raymond aren't big cake lovers. Well they used to like cake. It could well be they are playing down the love of cakes because if I know they love it, I would make one every week!"

Kissing them goodbye, Mrs G said, "Thanks for a lovely afternoon and dinner. See you tomorrow Jenny".

"You're very welcome", said Raymond.

The week was frantic for the couple. Merla had deadlines at work and Raymond was involved in a project, which needed completing by the end of the week. As he was the Accounts Manager, he oversaw the entire projects and needed to present to his boss to read over the weekend. It was a tight schedule, but that was life. The pressure on both of them meant Mrs Green fed Jenny and she did her homework at her house, so when she was collected, she would just be ready to shower and go to bed. Jenny was now nearly self-sufficient and she didn't need to be told what needed doing. Being an only child, she was very independent and she was becoming more grown up.

"The work Cyril is giving me is getting so challenging; I sometimes feel inept, constantly asking him questions. I am sure he thinks I am already a solicitor", moaned Merla.

"But it would be like that love. You need to be involved in difficult work now and the more you keep doing it, the easier it will become. You are not going to wake up one morning as a solicitor and then you start getting challenging work. That would be a nightmare for you. I'm sure with time all these difficult projects/cases will become easier for you".

"It's a good job my company is large and well structured so I have all the resources to hand and I am lucky to have a great boss who doesn't mind my asking questions. He's lovely", said Merla.

"You'll be fine", said Raymond reassuringly.

Jenny butted in here and said, "You always tell me mum, you won't succeed without hard work".

"I'm glad you were listening to me young lady!"

They all laughed as they said goodnight to Jenny.

The night when the couple went to bed, Raymond told Merla they needed to review insurance policies. He wanted to make sure both she and him were financially secure for Jenny if anything should happen to either of them. He researched and decided he wanted to increase the policies they already had. Typical Raymond, the next day he contacted his insurance company and increased the policies.

"You know Mrs G is right, let's make a date for the end of the month to do something - just you and I. We should go somewhere. I couldn't tell the last time we danced. In fact I think it was at our wedding and honeymoon." said Merla.

"OK Mrs Wilson, you tell me what you want us to do and I will oblige."

"No, let's decide together. What do you want to do? My immediate thought is to stay overnight in a hotel in London, book a table for a meal and go to either the theatre or a nightclub to dance", said Merla.

"OK, get Mrs G's and Jenny's approval and I'll book."

The following weeks went quickly and as promised at the end of the month the couple booked into a hotel in the centre of the West End of London. They decided to go to a club, which played '70s/80s soul music. They thought that would attract people of similar age and they were not disappointed, although to their surprise there were a few young people there who liked that era music. The music could not have been better with Stevie Wonder, Marvin Gaye, Harold Melvin & the Blue Notes and The Stylistics blasting. They then went to the restaurant downstairs to have a meal. The couple exchanged jokes, laughed, and then resumed dancing. As they danced to Billy Paul's song, they sang to each other and changed the words from "Me and Mrs Jones" into "Me & Mrs Wilson, We have a thing going on". They laughed as they tried to force a two-syllable word into a one syllable. The evening ended with them returning to the hotel and making love, falling asleep like babies, getting up late in the morning, having breakfast and then leaving the hotel. On their way home, they strolled through Hyde Park and both kissed and thanked each other for a great weekend.

"We'll have to do this again soon darling," said Raymond.

CHAPTER 6

Winter had now passed and spring was now here. Into the year, Merla was at the end of her training contract.

As she had worked in so many departments, she was now equipped to work in most departments in the company. She was so happy and relieved that she had accomplished her dream of becoming a solicitor. She could not thank Cyril enough and insisted on taking him to lunch as a way of thanking him and to tell him about her plans. He always looked out for her and said he would let her know when a vacancy came up for a more challenging role within the company.

"You know you are like my guardian angel. I cannot tell you how grateful I am for all you have done for me. You have helped me to achieve my dream and make my family so proud of me. Thank you so much", she said to Cyril.

"Not at all, I saw a lot of potential in you and everyone needs a leg up. I could see talent and I am not surprised you have made it. We all know what it takes to go the route you have gone, but I could see the way you worked hard, you had a stoic determination. Well done!"

That evening she went home she rang Aunt Bess to tell her the good news that she was now a fully qualified solicitor.

"Uncle Harry would have been so proud of you! Your mother would have been also so proud! I'm sure she is looking down on you now. We are all very proud of you. You are an inspiration to Eddie, Gloria, and Jenny. Great News! Well done love!"

Raymond then phoned his mother and father to tell them the good news.

The weekend included a celebratory dinner with Jenny, Mrs Green, Raymond, and Merla. They could not exclude Mrs Green, as she was so supportive to Merla from day one. It was also an acknowledgement, to confirm appreciation for all she had done for the couple and to confirm her status in the family.

Raymond said to Merla, "As promised, I am going to invite the family and close friends for dinner. It's all going to be on me so I will book a table at our favourite restaurant. You don't worry I will arrange, just tell me who you want to invite and when to have it".

"We should definitely invite Ruth and Monty, and of course Mrs Green. I'll let you have details of a couple more people to invite. Apart from that, it is your family, as I don't have many friends or family over here. I should imagine the maximum should be around 20/30 people, don't you think?" asked Merla.

"It's got to be weekend love and particularly a Saturday evening, as most people are at work in the week. It also has to be at about 7.30/8.00pm as most Saturdays mornings/early afternoons are spent shopping and doing household chores. Can I leave that with you?" asked Merla.

"Of course - will let you have details once I have organised. Don't worry your pretty little head", he said with a smile.

Jenny was growing up fast now, and being at secondary school she had her own friends and was more independent. She wanted the kind of freedom that her friends enjoyed but her parents were much more strict than their parents were. Her parents were less enthusiastic about letting go and were interested in whom she associated with, although they didn't make it obvious.

Merla got a promotion within her company after a year's qualifying, thanks to Cyril telling her about the position. She was no longer in his department although they still spoke, especially if she was in doubt, she felt confident and comfortable enough to phone or go into his office for advice, although not often as Merla wanted to stand on her own two feet. He had already been so helpful. This meant they were more better off financially and they decided they wanted to start their family as Merla was now nearly 32 and although she was still within childbearing age, she was aware that Jenny was alone and wanted to give her a brother or sister before she became too old to care about big sister responsibilities.

One day Raymond came home to hear some very good news.

"You'd never guess what? You are going to be a dad… for real". Merla was indeed three months pregnant. She didn't want to say anything before just in case she got the dates wrong.

"Oh my God, thank you so much Lord. That is wonderful news darling". He hugged and kissed her. "I am so happy. You have done well Mrs Wilson. You are making me so very happy darling".

She announced it to Jenny, Mrs G and her work colleagues. They were not surprised as she hinted to her associates that they were hoping to increase the family soon. Those who knew her felt she would cope as Raymond was there for her.

In the early stages, she had morning sickness but as the months went by, her bump grew, but she was still coping with the hectic workload although by the time she got home she was exhausted. Merla ambled home and could no longer run down the escalator. Jenny was now prepared for big sister responsibilities and was helping more without being asked to do household tasks. Raymond took on more household responsibilities and sometimes he worked from home, which meant he didn't have to commute and be at a desk every day.

One evening Merla came home to see Raymond lying on the sofa and this was unlike him. He had collected Jenny but he felt sick. There was an unusual pain in his stomach even though he had taken some indigestion tablets. He thought it was something he had eaten but the stomach pain was not going away.

"What's the matter darling?"

"I don't know I have had a pain in my stomach and it doesn't seem to be shifting. I kept trying to ignore it and thought it may be trapped wind, heartburn, indigestion, but I am not sure now. It's not going away."

"Do you want a cup of tea, some hot drink to see if it goes? If it gets worse, let's take you to the hospital as it's too late for the GP. I will ask Mrs Green to come round as Jenny is nearly ready for bed. I'm sure she won't mind".

The pain wasn't dissipating so Merla collected Mrs Green while Raymond got ready for the hospital and she dropped her off and picked up Raymond.

With a worried look on her face as she drove him she said, "So how long have you had this pain?"

"I don't really know. I thought what I was feeling was just indigestion which I sometimes used to get. I then felt it was heartburn and that is why I was becoming more conscious about eating spicy food. You know me, I tend to ignore illnesses, like headaches and colds thinking that the body will fight off whatever ailments it faces. In the past it's worked for me but this one doesn't feel right".

"OK love don't worry we are nearly there and hopefully it's a simple answer to a simple problem. The trouble is with neither of us having any medical knowledge we could be worrying in vain. In fact I refuse to believe anything else but that we are worrying unnecessarily!" said Merla.

They had private medical insurance but went to the Accident and Emergency Department. They were completely unaware how long this would take, as there were a few people in the waiting room.

"We are here now so we might as well wait". Merla waited for nearly an hour and went up to the nurse, explaining to her that her child was at home with a babysitter who couldn't stay indefinitely. Could she give them some idea when they would see a doctor?

Nonchalantly the nurse retorted, "There is nothing I can do about it; it depends on each person's illness and there are only a few doctors on duty tonight. Sorry".

"Look, I am pregnant as you can see and I am tired and haven't eaten since this morning!".

"There is a café down the bottom of the corridor. You may be able to get a sandwich and hot drink from the machine. I cannot do any more. Can you imagine if I let your husband through before the other patients how furious people would be? Everybody's case is urgent!"

Merla went outside to calm down and phoned Mrs Green to tell her she didn't know what time she would be returning.

"Don't worry yourself about what time you return. I know I haven't worked for a while, but hospitals are always like this. If anything, I'll just rest on the sofa until you people return. Jenny is already in bed hopefully sleeping."

"I didn't know that it was like this in the Accident and Emergency Dept. What has happened to the NHS? First thing tomorrow, I will be contacting BUPA if we don't get a sensible answer tonight. Just want them to answer why he is feeling such pain or at least to stop the ache. See you later and thanks again."

The couple waited a long while and then saw a nurse who asked him some relevant health questions. Raymond eventually saw a doctor, who checked over him. He then gave him some painkillers to get rid of the pain and suggested he made an appointment to see his GP the next day if the pain persisted.

The next day he went to his GP who examined him again and after asking him several questions, he recommended further tests.

Merla didn't sleep very well as she was very worried about Raymond. They were not naive and if the GP could not diagnose the problem at the visit, they knew something was seriously wrong. To support him and to convince herself, she was outwardly positive and appeared calm. She prayed fervently asking God to take away the pain, and heal him from whatever he had wrong with him. She did try to Google his complaint but the prognosis could have been anything, so that wasn't helpful. In fact, it made matters worse as she kept thinking the worse. She dared not contemplate any problem with his health, as their life as a family was just beginning.

Now using private medical insurance, Raymond had an x-ray very quickly. The specialist recommended he should also have an endoscopy test, with the endoscope passing down the gullet into the stomach so the specialist could look for any unusual signs. They would also take a biopsy of the tissues.

The specialist asked him to come in for the results. Merla accompanied her husband. As they entered the room, they sensed it was bad news as a couple of other medical people were in the room.

The doctor said, "We have had your test results back and the result is not an ulcerated stomach but is in fact a malignant tumour in the stomach. The problem was it could initially be mistaken as heartburn or indigestion, so please do not be too hard on yourself for not coming to see us earlier. This is relatively unusual for a person your age, but it is still possible. I am sorry to have to give you this news. I believe we have caught it early and although we cannot guarantee the outcome, we are hopeful".

He added that there would be a team of specialists working with him so he wouldn't be making all the decisions on his own. He went through the scan with the couple and asked, "Have you any questions?"

Merla wasn't stupid, she knew it was stomach cancer and numbed by the prognosis, she said nothing. Tears just ran down her face and her crying became uncontrollable. She used up the obligatory box of tissues on the doctor's desk.

Raymond asked with total resignation the following questions: "At what stage is the cancer? What treatment do you recommend? What will be the process now we know what it is and when will I have the operation?"

"It was Stage 1/early Stage 2" was the response, recommending an operation. The doctor added, "If you prefer you can have a second opinion. Going private means you can choose the hospital, the specialists and the time of your choice. If you like, we can perform the operation next week. I am not the only doctor involved; we are a team: myself - the surgery oncologist, the anaesthetist, the gastroenterologist, radiation and medical oncologists, and of course the specialist nurses and hospital technicians. You are a priority because of the diagnosis. From the scan we can identify the problem, and we shall do everything possible to achieve a positive outcome, but of course we cannot guarantee 100% success as it depends on the individual and what we find, but we have done this type of surgery several times before so we are confident there is every chance of success".

The next few days were anxious and Merla preoccupied herself supporting Raymond spiritually, mentally and physically. She completely put her pregnancy issues, like feeling tired, on hold, as this now seemed insignificant. She made phone calls to her family abroad and to Raymond's family, explaining the prognosis, with the help of her nurse friend, Ruth. Merla took charge of supporting Raymond, Jenny, Aunt Bess, and Raymond's family. Her friends now rallied round her. His parents were also shocked and being unfamiliar with medical issues, the news about cancer seemed like the worse news they could have received, as they were from the generation where cancer spells death.

In order not to delay the operation, the couple decided against a second opinion but to go ahead with the oncologist surgeon they saw. With all the preparation in place, the surgeon said his team could operate next Monday. That was the longest five days for the family, who now wanted to get this sorted out as soon as possible. Raymond's family and church family prayed emphatically and by the time the day came, they were prepared mentally and spiritually. Raymond was calm. His faith was strong and he felt God would be with him during this difficult time.

They arrived the night before the operation, as he was first on the list. On the morning, Merla was distressed but was calm outwardly to support her husband. During the operation, she sat quietly in the reception area with

Raymond's mother and father. Magazines spread over the table varied from angling to yoga. The room was so quiet that the only sound heard was from the leaves of the magazine pages as Merla flicked the pages over. It was obvious that she was not reading anything because of the frequency of the flips. Now and again, they had a cup of water from the machine to pass the time.

After several anxious hours, the operation was over but it was too early to tell whether it was successful or not. It would take another 24-48 hours at least to see if the operation was a success. Merla could not yet see her husband, as he was still unconscious but now in the Recovery Room, with tubes coming from his mouth and nose, and linking to machines. Silently they waited for him to become conscious. He started to recover but as the anaesthetic was wearing off, he was still in pain and feeling a lot of discomfort even although the post-operative staff monitored and ordered analgesic drug. As his situation did not improve and looked as if he was deteriorating, they called for the specialists to investigate. Outside of the Recovery Room, the surgeon who operated updated Merla and family and advised that they needed to take him back into surgery, as there appeared to be complications following the operation.

An hour later, the team came out to give the family the news that Raymond unfortunately did not make it as there were complications, with unusual amount of bleeding and try as they might, they were unsuccessful in saving his life.

"What are you saying? My husband is dead?" Merla asked.

"Yes" said the doctor calmly. "We are extremely sorry to have to deliver this news to you. We did everything we could but ……..".

Before he could finish what he was saying, his sentence was interrupted with a torrent of hysterical wailing. The room changed from silence to a chorus of unimaginable bawling. His parents froze in disbelief.

"Can I get you a drink?" one hospital staff asked.

"No thanks", they said.

Confusion set in. They did not know who or what to blame for this calamitous unbelievable news. In fact, it would have been easier to blame someone, but that would not help to bring Raymond back to life. In no time at all paper tissues filled the nearby bins. When the tears subsided, they washed their faces and called close family and friends with the dreadful news. They called Ruth and the rest of the family from hospital. Ruth left work immediately and arrived at the hospital to comfort Merla and get further details as to what happened.

Coping with pregnancy and not having eaten the entire day, the operation and the news, she was exhausted and shattered, but she rang Mrs Green to give her the news, but asked her not to say a word to Jenny, as she wanted to tell her personally.

Mrs Green promised her not to say anything, but Jenny could detect a changing tone in her voice and persona when Mrs G finished speaking to her mother.

"What's the matter ? Was that my mum?"

"Yes, it was - she just phoned to say she will be home soon. OK love?"

As an excuse, and to avoid any more questions from Jenny, Mrs Green went out of the room into the kitchen to wash the dishes and she quietly prayed for the family.

"My God, how could you let this happen? What is going to happen to Raymond's wife and his unborn baby? How could you do this Lord? Why, oh why, they were such a lovely family, just starting to live a fulfilled life. He was your child, they believed in you. I sometimes do not understand your ways Lord. Why, oh why did you allow this to happen? Why is our faith being tested in such a way?"

Merla could not drive, so she left her car at the hospital and Ruth took Raymond's parents and Merla home. Ruth phoned her husband Monty to pick up Merla's car while she stayed with Merla.

On reaching home, Merla went into Jenny's bedroom and told her the bad news.

"I have some sad news to tell you my love. Daddy had his operation this morning, but he didn't make it; unfortunately, he died after the operation due to severe bleeding and complications. I am so sorry to have to tell you this". Merla tried hard not to burst out into tears again as she wanted to be strong for her daughter.

"Daddy has died?" Jenny asked in a questioning tone. When the answer sunk in, the sobbing went from discreet to unmanageable bawling. Crying is infectious but all understood these tears and now Merla joined her. Ruth and Mrs Green came into her room, trying to help Merla to console her. Ruth thought, "How do you help a child to come to terms with the loss of a loved one. A father she now had. It's hard enough for the adult, let alone a child."

Mrs Green offered to stay with Merla the next few days to comfort and help her, if only to listen to her when she was feeling down and wanted to talk to someone and Merla accepted.

Mrs Green prepared a light supper for Merla and Jenny stayed up later as she was not going to school the next day. She was however tired so her mother asked her to get some rest even if she did not feel like sleeping.

In the living room, Merla cried again. All sorts of emotions surfaced that evening: sadness, anger, regret, blame, and despondency. Not knowing how or what to do or say, Mrs Green asked:

"Can I pray for you and the family?"

Merla shouted, "No! No! I don't want any more prayers! I don't believe a God we - especially Raymond - followed and trusted, how could He do that to us? We had so much faith in Him and He has destroyed our lives by taking Raymond away from us! It's like the moment I was given happiness,

God snatched it out of my hands! Poor Jenny, hasn't and didn't know a father! She gained a good father and now he's been taken from her. Life is so unfair."

Mrs Green had never seen Merla so angry. She just hugged Merla and Jenny without saying another word.

Merla was so tired; she had a shower and went into her bedroom. She did not sleep immediately as Mrs Green could hear her crying. Eventually she did fall asleep from the bad news and tiredness of the day.

Mrs Green cried quietly and prayed to God asking Him to help Merla through this difficult period. She fell asleep eventually after reading her favourite passages in the Bible including Psalms 28 and 31:1-18; Hebrews 11 and 12 and by the time she got to Job, she fell asleep.

Merla was exhausted the next day but she had to do certain things: first, she phoned her work and told them the sad news. She had not yet started maternity leave, although she was nearly 8 months pregnant. Before Raymond's illness, she thought she could work a couple more weeks as she felt all right albeit tired in the evenings. She would not now be at work for a while. She was also in touch with funeral parlours and Raymond's parents about the church service and other issues. His family was devastated. In fact, they were not much help to her in their shock. The church was not only shocked, they couldn't believe the news: a couple of weeks ago what they perceived as a healthy looking man and the next news they are hearing about his demise.

They told all the families abroad but because of exams for Eddie and Gloria, Aunt Bess and none of her overseas families would be attending. The reality was also the unexpected expense for the cost of travelling again for the three of them. In the final analysis, Merla would have paid for their fares, but she preferred if they came after she gave birth. The funeral went ahead the following week: two weeks before Merla's delivery date.

The night before the funeral, Raymond's parents invited church friends round their house to celebrate Raymond's life. Merla didn't attend as she had so many loose ends to tie up, plus she was exhausted. She would not want to let down Raymond, as he was such an organised person. Paradoxically, he would not want anything to happen to his unborn child so she was now more aware of the baby. Although she had sorted Uncle Harry's funeral, she had forgotten how much arrangement a funeral entailed. She had support, but ultimately she needed to make the final decision. Every time the baby moved or kicked in her stomach, she cried, thinking how Raymond would not be around to share in the joy.

On the day of the funeral, everything went smoothly. Surprisingly she was composed but cried demurely. Giving the church folks credit, they were active in choosing the hymns and passages from the Bible. They also organised the food as they had some idea of the numbers of the congregation that would be attending. Everyone just had to turn up for the funeral. It was a lovely sunny day, and if it wasn't for the fact that the occasion was a funeral, with the attire being black or dark clothing, and people crying, it was a celebration of a life. Merla requested a few of Raymond's favourite songs to be played after the funeral when people sat down to eat, but she refused to have any of their intimate love songs. The saddest and unbearable part of the day was the actual burial, with the body going down into the ground. At one point during that part of the burial, after she threw in a red rose, she left to sit in the car to cry alone. Ruth followed her while Mrs Green kept an eye on Jenny. After her tears had subsided, she reflected on the day and her current experience to Ruth saying.

"It was so lovely to see how human beings are so kind; they go out of their way to comfort and help without even being asked in a crisis. I am surrounded by a wonderful set of people. Thanks for being there for us".

Merla cried herself to sleep every night after the funeral. The baby was active. As she laid in bed, with the baby moving about and kicking, she would look at her stomach and wondered about Raymond and what he would be saying or doing at that time when a leg or an arm popped up to transform her bulk. Now and again, she smiled to herself as her stomach ebbed and flowed as she changed position.

In the final week of her pregnancy, she arranged for someone to pick up

Aunt Bess, Gloria, and Eddie from the airport. They arrived just in time to see the birth of a lovely healthy baby girl. Merla's immediate response when she saw her baby girl was to wonder if she looked like her father or her. She took features from both of them: Her mother's mouth and nose, her father's eyes and long fingers. Although she and Raymond spoke about names, they hadn't yet decided on a name. She cried and involuntarily said to Raymond "Here is your daughter darling". She felt his presence with her at the birth and she felt he was looking at the baby and her at that moment.

Aunt Bess looked on as she spoke to Raymond. It may seem strange to some people but as these were religious people, they believed in the afterlife and spirits; not in a macabre way, but in a positive way.

The family went home the next day with the baby. Typical Raymond, he planned for the unexpected and although he didn't expect to die, it did cross his mind, like most human beings, that his demise was a possibility. He paid the local florist money for flowers to be delivered to his wife. The next-door neighbour knocked on the door with a beautiful bunch of flowers delivered while they were away. On the greeting tag was a message from Raymond, saying

"Just in case anything happened to me,
look after yourself and our family and be strong.
I love you so much - Love you always. Your husband Raymond xx "

She cried. The whole situation was surreal, poignant, and confusing.

When Merla composed herself, she thanked Aunt Bess that she could be with them and the support she was giving them. She would be there with them for three weeks as the Gloria and Eddie needed to get back to their education.

"I don't know what I would do without you ". Jenny was now back at school after the birth so Aunt Bess helped to get her ready, but as she was now a big girl, Jenny was now coming home on her own as her mother was at home.

Every time she passed the bouquet of flowers displayed on the mantelpiece, she remembered Raymond and she either cried or smiled. Smiled as she thought that was typically Raymond to think of everything. He was so caring, loving, and thoughtful and she now refused to contemplate her future without him. She took one day at a time. She cried as she was missing him.

Merla had forgotten how much work was involved in looking after a baby. She now coped so much better as she was older and wiser but it was still hard work, especially without her husband.

As time passed she realised it was nearly time for Aunt Bess to return home. She may not realise but her presence helped Merla to deflect attention from her loss.

On the day to return home Merla dropped them off at the airport, asking Mrs. Green to keep the baby, who Merla named Sarah Louise Wilson. She was going to miss them greatly but promised as soon as she could, she would visit them.

As the days and weeks passed by Merla took the opportunity to spend more time with Sarah and Jenny. She walked through the local park nearly every day, sometimes with Mrs Green and sometimes on her own.

As the autumn arrived, she noticed leaves falling to the ground and she reflected how this was the same for human beings: 'Everything there is a season' (Ecclesiastes 3). She then started to sing The Byrds song, *'Turn, Turn, Turn'* but she could not get past 'A time to be born, and a time to die'. She cried as she made her way home and as a woman approached her, she stopped and carried on as if something was in her eyes. She then remembered Raymond's words about being strong, straightened herself, and walked home quickly. Yes, life goes on regardless.

- End -

RECIPES IN
"MEET ME AT HEAVEN'S GATE"

JERK PORK OR JERK CHICKEN

Ingredients

- 2 onions, peeled and chopped
- 2 garlic cloves peeled and crushed
- 4 tablespoons lime juice
- 2 tablespoon each dark molasses, soy sauce, chopped fresh root ginger
- 2 jalapeño chillies, deseeded and chopped
- 1/2 tsp each ground allspice (ground pimento) and ground nutmeg
- 4 pork chops or 4 chicken breast/thighs
- Sprigs of fresh parsley to garnish (Serves 4)

Method

- To make the jerk pork marinate, puree the onion, garlic, lime juice, molasses, soy sauce, ginger, chilli, cinnamon, allspice and nutmeg together in a food processor until smooth. Put the pork chops into a dish and pour over the marinade, turning the chops to coat. If using a pork shoulder, make shallow cuts and rub in. Marinade in the refrigerator for about 1 hour or overnight.

- Heat the griddle pan until almost smoking. Remove the pork chops from the marinade, scraping off any surplus and add to the hot pan. Cook for 10-15 minutes or until completely softened. Garnish with fresh parsley. Jerk Pork is best when grilled over branches of pimento (allspice) wood, but tasty even when cooked over charcoal or in the oven.

ACKEE & SALT FISH

Ingredients

- 2 dozen ackees
- 1 lb salt fish
- 4 rashers streaky bacon
- 2 medium onions
- Few blades of scallion
- 2 tablespoons butter or olive oil
- Piece of hot pepper
- 1/2 green pepper
- Black pepper (pinch)

Method

- Boil fish after soaking in cold water to remove salt. Flake.
- Remove ackees from pods, seeds and red centre (if not already done).
- Wash and put into cold water. Boil for 15 minutes.
- Place butter or oil into frying pan and fry bacon. Softly fry onions, scallion, and green pepper until soft or slightly brown.
- Add flaked fish and cooked ackees to frying pan, with fried onions etc.
- Gently stir and add black pepper.

Rice and Peas

Ingredients

- 6 oz dried red kidney bean
- 1 tsp vegetable oil
- 1 onion peeled and finely chopped
- 3 garlic cloves, peeled, and crushed
- 2 bay leaves, fresh if possible
- 8 oz long grain white rice
- 1/2 tin coconut milk
- 6 fl oz chicken or ham stock (optional)
- Sprig of thyme
- Small piece of Scotch bonnet pepper (optional)

Method

- Place washed beans in a large saucepan with 2 litres cold water. Bring to the boil and continue boiling gently until the beans are soft. Add more water if necessary.
- Season the beans with the onions, garlic, bay leaves, coconut milk, chicken stock, thyme.
- Cover and gently cook for a further 5 minutes.
- Ensure the peas and stock tasty as this will determine how the rice and peas will taste.
- Add the washed rice to the pot. Cover and allow to steam over a very low heat until cooked.

Boiled Yellow Yam

Ingredients

- 3 pounds yellow yam
- 1 teaspoon salt (optional)
- 1 teaspoon vegetable oil (optional)

Method

- Peel yam, Place in boiling water
- Cook until soft

BOILED DUMPLINGS

Ingredients

- 2 cups plain flour
- 1.5 teaspoon salt
- 1/4 cup cornmeal
- 1/2 cup cold water

Method

- Sift the flour, cornmeal, and salt together into a large mixing bowl. Add the water 3 teaspoons at a time, just enough to bring the dough together with a firm consistency.

- On a lightly floured surface, knead the dough well, for about five minutes.

- Boil a pot with water

- Break off pieces and form the dough into slightly flattened biscuits, about 2 inches across. For spinners roll the pieces between your palms into a pen shape.

- Place the pieces, uncrowded, into the pot of hot water –(Approx 5 -8 minutes). Serve hot with other food (Serves 6-8)

Pumpkin Soup

Ingredients

- 5 cup(s) water
- 2 1/2 pound(s) pumpkin, large diced
- 4 cup(s) chicken stock
- 3 clove(s) garlic, chopped
- 1 stalk(s) escallion, chopped
- 1 large onion, chopped
- 1 sprig(s) thyme
- 1 whole scotch bonnet pepper
- 1 tablespoon(s) Butter or Margarine
- 1 1/4 teaspoon(s) salt

Method

- In a saucepan bring to a boil 5 cups of water.
- Peel and dice pumpkin, add to boiling water and cook until tender.
- Drain and set aside to cool.
- Blend pumpkin using 4 cups of chicken stock, and a packet of soup.
- Pour blended mixture into saucepan and bring to a boil.
- Add chopped garlic, escallion, onion, thyme, scotch bonnet pepper, Butter or Margarine and salt.
- Allow to cook for 10 minutes or until soup thickens
- **To Serve:** Soup may be served with slices of garlic bread.

Mackerel and Green Bananas

Ingredients

- 1 large smoked mackerel
- 1 onion
- 1 sprig scallion
- 1 small paprika
- 1 tomato
- 2 tablespoon cooking oil
- 1 teaspoon Caribbean seasoning or Jerk seasoning
- 1 teaspoon thyme
- 4 green bananas (or as required)

Method

- Boil the mackerel until most of the salt is gone (ensuring there remains some salt but not tasteless)
- In a frying pan fry sliced onions, scallion, paprika, tomato.
- Add mackerel, seasoning and thyme
- In a separate pot, peel green bananas and boil until cooked
- Serve - enough for 2 people. Can also be served with dumplings and boiled yam.

Spaghetti Bolognese

Ingredients

- 2 medium onions, peeled and chopped
- 1 tsp olive oil
- 2 garlic cloves, peeled and crushed
- 500g lean minced beef
- 1 tsp dried oregano or mixed herbs
- 400g can tomatoes or chopped tomatoes
- 300ml hot beef stock
- 1 tsp tomato ketchup or purée
- 1 tsp Worcestershire sauce
- Salt and ground black pepper
- 350g spaghetti
- Freshly grated Parmesan

Method

- Put the onion and oil in a large pan and fry over a fairly high heat for 3-4 mins. Add the garlic and mince and fry until they both brown. Add the herbs, and cook for another couple of minutes.

- Stir in the tomatoes, beef stock, tomato ketchup or purée, Worcestershire sauce and seasoning. Bring to the boil, then reduce the heat, cover and simmer, stirring occasionally, for 30 mins.

- Meanwhile, cook the spaghetti in a large pan of boiling, salted water, according to packet instructions. Drain well, run hot water through it, put it back in the pan and add a dash of olive oil, if you like, then stir in the meat sauce.

- Serve in hot bowls and hand round Parmesan cheese, for sprinkling on top.

Jamaican Beef Patty

Ingredients

Pastry

- 1lb plain flour
- 1 Teaspoon of curry powder (level of hotness as per choice)
- 1 Teaspoon of baking powder
- 1 tsp salt
- 1 Teaspoon turmeric
- 1/2 cup ice cold water
- 1/2 cup melted butter
- 1/2 cup shortening

Filling

- 1 medium onion, chopped
- 4 scallions, chopped
- 1 pound ground beef
- 2 teaspoons thyme
- 1 scotch bonnet pepper (Can be replaced by 1 tablespoon each curry powder / turmeric/chilli sauce)
- 2 garlic cloves
- Salt and black pepper, as per taste
- 1 teaspoon paprika
- 1/2 teaspoon sugar
- 1 teaspoon nutmeg
- 1/2 cup breadcrumbs
- 1 cup water

Method

Prepare the pastry

- Take a large mixing bowl and sieve the flour in it. Add the curry powder, baking powder, some salt and a pinch of turmeric and mix them well.

- Add butter and shortenings to form a mixture resembling breadcrumbs.

- Pour in some water and knead dough out of it, slightly sticky is good enough.

- Roll the dough with both the hands, and wrap it using a cling film and leave it to refrigerate for an hour.

Prepare the filling

- Heat some oil in a pan and stir fry the chopped onions and scallions in it.

- Before they start to turn brown in colour, add grounded beef along with some thyme, bonnet peppers, curry, turmeric, garlic, etc. Sprinkle some salt and pepper along with paprika and some sugar.

- Sprinkle some nutmeg powder and mix it well.

- Continue to fry until the mixture starts to turn dry.

- Mix in the breadcrumbs and some water (if required). Cook it while stirring till the mixture gets a thick and saucy consistency.

- Remove from flame and keep it aside to let it cool.

Assembling the patties

- Sprinkle some flour on a rolling board and with the help of a rolling pin, roll the pastry dough (about 1/8th of an inch in thickness)

- Cut out uniform sized circles from the rolled dough.

- Take a spoonful of the filling and place it on a single side of the circle. Do not take too much of the filling as that might cause trouble while cooking the pastries.

- Wet your fingers with some water and move them over the edges of each patty to moisten them a bit.

- Fold the pastry by rolling the empty side over the filled one, and shape it like a crescent. The pastry should be rolled in such a way that the edges are sealed the filling can't come out.

- If needed, gently press the edges of the sealed patty with your fingers or a spoon.

Baking the patties

Set the oven to preheat at 375 degrees.

Place aluminium foil in a baking dish and arrange the patties in it.

Let them bake for 30-35 minutes till they turn golden brown.

Once done, serve hot.

Cornmeal Porridge

Ingredients

- 2 1/2 cups cold Milk
- 1/2 cup cornmeal
- 2 cinnamon sticks
- 1/2 tsp Salt
- 1/2 tsp ground nutmeg
- 1/2 tsp Pimento berries (Optional)
- 2 tsp Vanilla Extract
- 2 tsp Condensed Milk (or more depending on how sweet preferred)
- 1 tsp Sugar

Method

- Pour milk into a saucepan over Medium-high heat
- Stir in cornmeal, cinnamon, salt, nutmeg and pimento
- Continue stirring until mixture starts to thicken and smooth
- Stir in vanilla, condensed milk and sugar
- Lower heat and stir until porridge is thick and creamy
- Remove cinnamon sticks and pimento berries and pour into bowls
- Makes 2 servings

LEMON DRIZZLE CAKE

Ingredients

- 225 g butter, softened
- 400 g caster sugar
- 3 lemons, finely grated zest only
- 4 large eggs
- 375 g self raising flour
- 200 ml milk

For the glaze

- 3 lemons, juice only
- 200g granulated sugar

Method

For the cake: preheat the oven to 180C/gas 4. Grease and flour a 25cm bun tin or regular cake tin.

Cream the butter and sugar with the lemon zest until pale and thick. Beating the lemon zest will help draw out the oil making the cake lovely and lemony.

Stir in the eggs, one at a time. If the mixture threatens to curdle, add a tablespoon of the flour to stabilise it.

Mix in a little of the flour with alternate glugs of the milk until all the ingredients are incorporated. (You may not always need to use all the milk)

Spoon the mixture into the baking tin and bake for 1 hour or until a toothpick inserted into the centre comes out clean. Cool in the tin for 10 minutes before turning out onto a rack. Prick all over with a knife or toothpick.

For the glaze: mix the lemon juice and sugar, just swirling gently so the sugar doesn't completely dissolve.

Drizzle the lemon glaze all over the warm cake - it will seep into the holes leaving a delicate sugar crust on the surface.

Sweet Potato Pudding

Ingredients:

- 2 pounds sweet potato
- 1 cup flour
- 2 cups coconut milk
- 1 cups raisin (some used other dried fruits)
- 2 teaspoons vanilla
- 1- 1/2 teaspoon grated nutmeg
- 1 teaspoon mixed spice
- 1 cup brown sugar
- 1 teaspoon salt
- 1 teaspoon margarine

Method

- Wash and peel off the skin of the potatoes
- Wash again then grate
- Grate coconut, add water and squeeze juice through a strainer
- Blend flour, mixed spice (raisins etc), salt, and nutmeg.
- Combine this mixture with the grated potatoes and mix well
- Add sugar, fruits and coconut milk. Mix well.
- Grease pan, pour in batter, bake at 350 degrees F for 40-60 minutes or until done

Simple Jamaican Rum Punch (Sweet)

Ingredients

- 1 Cup lime or lemon juice
- 2 cups strawberry flavoured syrup (or other simple red coloured syrup)
- 3 cups Jamaican white rum
- 4 Cups Fruit Juice (Combine 2 cups Pineapple and 2 cups Orange Juice)

Method:

- Mix everything together in a punch bowl
- Taste and adjust.
- Garnish with slices of lime and/or pieces of pineapple
- Place in the refrigerator to chill. Ageing improves Rum
- Punch so we suggest refrigerate and serve after 2 hours
- Serve cold over ice.
- Serves: 10-12

Simple Jamaican Rum Punch (Strong)

Ingredients:

- 1 Cup lime or lemon juice
- 2 cups strawberry flavoured syrup (or other simple red coloured syrup)
- 3 Cups Fruit Juice (Combine 1 cup Pineapple and 2 cups Orange Juice
- 4 cups Jamaican white rum

Method:

- Mix everything together in a punch bowl
- Taste and adjust.
- Garnish with slices of lime and/or pieces of pineapple
- Place in the refrigerator to chill. Ageing improves Rum
- Punch so we suggest refrigerate and serve after 2 hours
- Serve cold over ice.
- Serves: 10-12

CARROT JUICE

Ingredients

- 2 pounds Carrots grated or chopped
- 4 or more cups water
- 1 can Condensed milk
- 1/2 teaspoons nutmeg/ cinnamon adjust to taste
- 1 teaspoon vanilla
- 1 tablespoon sugar
- Rum - add according to preference optional

Method

- Grate carrots
- Add water
- Strain and add condensed milk, nutmeg, cinnamon, sugar and rum
- Mix and serve with ice

Lemonade

Ingredients

- 6 lemons or lime
- 6 spoons sugar
- 4 or more cups water

Method

- Juice lemons
- Add sugar and water
- Mix and serve with ice

PIÑA COLADA

Ingredients

- 3 parts Pineapple juice (3 ozs)
- 1-2 part(s) white rum (1-2 oz)
- 1 oz coconut cream
- 1 cup crushed ice

Method

- Put 1 cup of crushed ice in a blender
- Add 1 oz. of coconut cream to the blender
- Add 2 oz. of white rum to the blender
- Add 3 oz. of pineapple juice to the blender
- Blend the ingredients together
- Pour the piña colada into a glass

CHRISTMAS FRUIT CAKE

Ingredients

- 1 lb dark sugar
- 1 lb butter
- 1 lb self raising flour
- 9 eggs, whipped with lemon juice
- 3 level teaspoon mixed spice
- 1 level teaspoon baking powder
- 2 teaspoon nutmeg
- 5 table spoons mixed soaked fruits
- Browning – enough until dark
- Drops almond essence
- Drops of vanilla essence
- Rum and brandy flavouring
- 2 table spoons of white rum

Method

- In a mixing bowl rub/mix the sugar and butter until completely smooth and sugar grains are all gone.
- Add whipped eggs to bowl.
- Add self raising flour with baking powder, nutmeg, and mixed spice.
- Continue mixing until all the ingredients are fully integrated.
- Add mixed fruits, browning, vanilla essence, brandy flavouring, rum
- Warm oven
- Place in a tin large enough to accommodate mixture.
- Bake in a warm oven at 100c for 1 hour.
- Check if cooked and if not cover and leave for a further ½ hour.
- Take out and leave to cool.